Fanita Moon Pendleton

Shoot First Ask Questions Never

Julie !   Much

Thank

for Supt

D0061661

Moon

Dedication

Dedicated to my son Brione Lamont Pendleton, my inspiration to be a better me.

Acknowledgments

God is good ALL THE TIME. This book has been a long time coming in my heart and I want to **thank my**

Little brother Leihei Emigli (BayBay/Mig) his unconditional love and encouragement are a constant

blessing, you can check out his work on emigliarts.com love you baby. Love also to my Sister- in law

Bumi and my nephew Leihei and niece Ayinke (lil moon).

I have to acknowledge my mother **Jessie Marie Davenport** who without even knowing it, she passed on a love of reading and artistic endeavors to her children.

Big hugs to my father **Lawrence S. Pendleton, III**. I love you.

Posthumously I have to acknowledge my Paternal Grandmother **Mary Lee Andrews-Pendleton-Johnson**.

I can't explain how much I miss her or how much she has meant in my life. Love you Grams.

Posthumously I would like to thank my example of who and what a man should be **Lawrence S. Pendleton II** my Paternal Grandfather. Love You Grandaddy!!!!!

I want to give a **shout out to my VA crew** for supporting me and listening to me when all I could talk about was my damn book: Kesi Simmons, Velnita Morrison, Patrick Phinizee, Antonio Laughton, Lucinda Britt, Michelle Taylor, Marisha Griffith, Tongia & Nasha Robertson and of course my son Brione Pendleton.

Shout out to Sandy Smith (Oakland CA/now Las Vegas) for believing in me and encouraging me.

Shout out to my uncles Larry Pendleton, Sr. (Norfolk, VA) **and Carl Pendleton, Sr**. (Tulsa OK) for always believing in me and holding me down. I have learned a lot from you guys. love ya.

Aunt **Mary Louise Pendleton-Carter** (Kileen TX) you remind me so much of Grams.

I love you and **Uncle Paul**.

CONNECT WITH ME ON

Facebook- Fanita Moon Pendleton

Twitter- Moon081471

Instagram- FanitaMoonPendleton

Email- www.urbanmoonbooksandmore@gmail.com

Website- www.urbanmoonbooksandmore.com

MOON

MOMMA'S BABIES

"Ughhh I can't take this anymore!!!!"

Jewel yelled at the top of her lungs, she was out of breath, sweating and facing what to her were the worst contractions ever. Her stomach felt as though it would burst open upon her next breath. Her intake of air came at a rapid pace and was just as quickly released as she steeled her resolve to introduce the Dunbar ladies into the world.

The delivery room was full of movement, nurses were checking machines, and Dr. Johansen was attempting to coax Jewel into relaxing and letting the process run its course. "Ok Mrs. Dunbar," he started with a soothing voice, "you are doing a wonderful job, just breathe as normally as possible and relax because these young ladies are not quite ready to come out to play yet." He smiled warmly, attempting to reassure her.

Jewel attempted to calm down and take Dr. Johansen's advice by breathing as normally as possible. She moved her eyes from left to right searching wildly around the room for the only person who could calm her nerves with just a wink; her husband. Her breathing began to return to normal as they made eye contact and in those eyes Jewel found peace. He gave her a reassuring wink and mouthed, "I love you." Jewel absorbed his strength and relaxed.

This day had been anticipated by Lawrence and Jewel Dunbar since the day they found out they were expecting. Today was the day they would hold their precious gifts of twin girls. They had spent tireless hours together shopping, redecorating, and child proofing their large upscale home. Nothing was too good for the bundles of joy that would soon fill their lives with laughter and responsibility.

Jewel was painfully excited as she glanced around the delivery room at all of the activity. She wanted to forget about the pain and only think about the look of pride on her husband's face when she first told him he was going to be a father.

Lawrence was relaxing on their massive deck which was surrounded by the Chesapeake Bay. He was in his favorite recliner double stuffed with cushions that enveloped his large frame. Shirtless, he had a glass of his favorite Ciroc Ultra-Premium, and the tempting sounds of the O'Jays played at a low level from the surrounding speakers. It was the perfect scenery to share their wonderful news. Jewel watched him from a distance inhaling the scent of his favorite cologne as she marveled at her blessings; her husband was the shit and there was no doubt about that. Jewel was wearing one of his t-shirts and nothing else as she strolled over to him and stood behind his chair and began to caress his massive shoulders kneading them to the beat of the smooth sounds filling the air. Lawrence reached around and grabbed his wife bringing her into his lap and in his sexy deep baritone asked, "What did I do to deserve the impromptu massage?"

He rubbed his wife's cheeks starring deep into her eyes causing a slight eruption in Jewel's sweet earth. "You deserve this and so much more," Jewel answered as she bent down and tasted her husband's tongue. She sucked the residue of Ciroc gently and rubbed her hands over his chest. Deciding to release his tongue from the prison of her mouth and replace it with his nipple, she used her tongue to trace around his nipple and bite gently.

She could feel his appreciation as it grew to full strength in his basketball shorts beneath her while she straddled his lap. Jewel began grinding in her husband's lap as his fingers traveled to her essence and disappeared inside of her soaked womanhood. "Ummmm baby you know I love the way you touch me," Jewel stated as she continued to grind harder to his drumbeat within her. His lap was soaked with her juices as he expertly pulled the t-shirt over her head and his shorts down while balancing Jewel on his lap and continuing to stroke the depths of her love spot. Jewel's eyes grew wide and her breath caught in her throat as her husband entered her, it never got any easier for her to take so much dick at one time, but she was always up for the task.

The sounds of ecstasy arising from Jewel were a direct result of the assault he was placing on her G-Spot as she bounced up and slammed back down on her dick over and over again, her firm ass slamming against his thick thighs. Her juices were flowing as her body began trembling. He tightened his grip on her waist and guided her down as he met her stroke for stroke.

He placed her nipples in his mouth moving from one breast to the other, continuing to dive deep into waters only he has navigated. The love making moved into overdrive as he dove deeper and deeper driving both to scream out their release in unison. Sweat dripped down their bodies and the cool breeze of the night now evident caused them to hold each other close as their breathing attempted to restore some sense of normalcy. It was in that moment Jewel looked into her husband's eyes and lowered herself for another kiss before pulling away from him and sitting up straight on his lap. Marvin Gay and Tammie Terrel's Ain't Nothing Like The Real Thang was playing making an already perfect scene even better as she let the words spill from her mouth, "We are going to be parents Lawrence." The smile in her eyes conveyed how happy she was to have his seeds growing inside of her womb, safe and secure, and was reflected in the ear to ear smile coming from her husband as he reached to pull her into the cradle of his arm and began speaking into her neck "Jewel I have never been so happy about anything in my life, and I swear to you I am going to be everything you and our children need." Facing him with tears sliding down her face Jewel nodded her head up and down "I have no doubt baby." They spent the rest of the evening in each other's arms on the deck of their home sharing thoughts of raising their own family

Jewel was jarred from her pleasant thoughts by another searing contraction which caused her to yell out and almost sit up in the birthing bed "Urgggggggggggggh Urgggggggggggggggggh shh shhh shh Urgggggggggggggg"

The screams came out in between bursts of breath which threatened to stop at any moment as she gripped the rails on the bed with her face contorting in pain. Lawrence rushed to her side as hospital staff scurried into place preparing for the birth of his seeds. He grabbed her left hand from the rail and encouraged her to squeeze his. His nearness calmed her some and her breathing began to regulate.

The pain was different now; it was more pronounced, sharper. It felt like her body was on fire and she thought these had to be the worst contractions ever. Jewel began to cry and reach out for her husband; she called him Lawrence, only she could get away with that, everyone else called him GOD.

When GOD heard his wife scream out for him he knew something was wrong. The beeping of machines and the urgent movement of the nurses and the doctor made him alert and worried for his wife, but it didn't show on his face. He stood strong for her, squeezing her hand and wiping her face off with a cool rag. He made eye contact with Dr. Johansen.

The look in his eye made Dr. Johansen nervous, he sensed danger. The doctor knew the look to be a threat meaning, *"If she dies, you die."* and with that he felt a different sense of urgency to ensure this birth went off without a hitch. The doctor was aware of the complications Jewel was experiencing and began to coax her through the delivery.

"Ok Mrs. Dunbar your princesses are ready to make their appearance. I want you to start to push." Dr. Johansen pleaded but tried to keep his voice soothing, *"There you go Mrs. Dunbar, you are almost there I can see a head."*

Jewel began to scream louder, her screams echoed off the walls of the delivery room and were filled with more pain than GOD could stand to hear from the only woman he had ever given his heart to. He wanted so badly to soothe her. He turned towards the doctor, "Do something now!" his tone was unmistakable.

Jewel yelled out again, "Oh my lord help me ...help ...help....help...."

She could feel the first baby's head as well; it felt as though she was being ripped in half. But that was not where the greatest pain was coming from. The pain was in her heart, it felt as though her heart was going to burst. She had a strange thought through the pain, it felt like Congo drums being beat by hundreds of drummers. She squeezed her husband's hand hard thinking surely she could transfer some of her pain to him. He could carry it for her as he had carried her pain in the past.

One of the nurses turned from the monitor to get Dr. Johansen's attention, "Doctor we are losing her!"

The heart monitor began to slow down and the doctor went into life-saving mode, but he had to choose, he could either save Jewel or save her unborn children.

Despite the dangerous vibes, Dr. Johansen was getting from GOD, he was determined to act professionally and Jewel was his patient.

Dr. Johansen looked at GOD and in a voice that belied his confidence he said, "Mr. Dunbar you have to make a decision. Which one I am going to save, your wife or your daughters?"

The lights in the room felt brighter than they actually were. The brightness was almost accusatory; like the light was pointing its finger at GOD. He had made many life and death decisions in the past, he either took life himself or gave the order for life to be taken. Why was he having such a hard time making this decision? GOD instantly knew this would be the hardest decision he would ever have to make. Sure they could have other children, but these were his seeds and he truly loved his unborn daughters. A loud scream from Jewel rocked GOD to his core; it made his insides feel like lava. He turned and looked into the face of the only woman he loved in life. In that moment his mind drifted back to an earlier time, the time when he first realized he was in love.

Lawrence spotted her sitting on the porch of her grandparents large Victorian home by herself in the Huntersville section of Norfolk, Virginia. Jewel had a familiar far out look on her face. Whenever he saw her sitting by herself he noticed this same look. The look both concerned and saddened him. He wanted to be the one to bring the light into Jewels eyes but he didn't know where the pain was coming from.

Lawrence never had much interaction with Jewel after he first spotted her on that porch but what he noticed even at 14 years old was Jewel was everything he could ever want in a mate. He wanted to protect her from the sadness in her eyes, a sadness he knew she was too beautiful and young to have. He knew from watching his father for years that the protective feelings he had for this girl who he hardly knew were signs of love. There were many occasions after he became infatuated with Jewel he jacked somebody up at school or in the neighborhood when he found out they were teasing Jewel. Needless to say she never knew why the teasing stopped, it just mysteriously did. To Lawrence, Jewel belonged to him. Her budding breast and shapely thighs may have caught his attention but her butter pecan skin and big wide eyes captured his heart. He promised himself he would be the one to erase the hurt from her eyes and replace it with something to make her natural beauty shine through.

"URRGGGhhh" Jewel's loud screeches brought GOD back from his memories and he could hear her calling for him "LAWRENCEEEEEEEEEE" He turned to her side grabbing her hand and kissing her ears telling her how much he loved her. What he heard next would change his life forever, the Jewel of his life whispered to him through clenched screams.

"Lawrence save the babies, save the babies."

God felt like his heart was about to leave his body, but with the demeanor that he is infamous for he looked at Dr. Johansen and said "Save my seeds."

GOD immediately bent down and breathed his last words in Jewel's ear, "Baby, I love you to life. I'm going to take good care of our ladies. I will make sure they are true to the game and they know you are watching over them." The room was filled with noise but in this moment GOD and Jewel found a quiet peace between themselves.

Jewel could feel herself slipping away from Lawrence. A tear rolled down her cheek as she looked into the eyes of the man who had literally breathed life back into her and healed her from the heartbreak of her parent's abandonment. She continued to push her children forward into the world determined to give something back to the man that had given her so much. .

Everything inside of GOD's brain and heart was vibrating beyond control, he was about to lose his soul mate, the only woman that truly understood him and loved him completely. God kissed Jewel's mouth just as he heard the sweetest cry he would ever hear. The wailing was Monique Shakira Dunbar coming into the world.

Lawrence and Jewel had pre-named the girls regardless of their birth order - didn't matter who came first, she would be Monique and the second would be Dominique.

Jewel heard the loud cry of her oldest daughter and the reality that she would never get to bath her, feed her, or teach her how to be a lady overwhelmed her and tears began to run from her eyes. She thought about the fact that she wouldn't be there to hear about her daughters' first crush, or their first heartbreak. The pounding in her heart was as real as if someone was beating on her chest. Every fiber of her body wanted the doctor to turn to her and say she would be fine, that her heart was not exploding out of her chest. She noticed the puzzled look on her husband's face and wondered if he would miss her, she knew her soul could rest because she had truly been loved.

GOD noticed he didn't hear another cry that would announce Dominique's arrival. He moved his lips from Jewel's and cast his icy gaze eyes down on the doctor. The thoughts running through his mind were on the females in his life, he was already losing Jewel, he could not lose Dominique too. When GOD looked over the doctor's shoulder and the nurses who were busy doing their job he realized Dominique Sierra Dunbar had in fact made her appearance, but she didn't cry out.

GOD made it over to the warming bed that held his daughters in one swift motion, his presence loomed over the nurses, intimidating them without even trying. The sound of his voice was demanding, the nurses could feel the depth of his soul as he fired off rapid questions,

"What's wrong with her? Why isn't she crying? She better be alright!"

Dr. Johansen was attempted to explain what was happening just as the monitors in the room began to chirp slower and slower until they all heard the ringing of the flat line. The tension in the room tripled. GOD didn't think he would ever forget the sound that signified his finest Jewel leaving this earth. Shedding tears was not an option right now. He loved Jewel but he knew she would want him to concentrate on their babies so he turned his attention to his daughters. He knew at this time they needed him and he needed to concentrate on them to get through this tragedy. He made his peace with Jewel but wondered if his heart would ever recover from losing her.

The doctor assured God, Dominique was perfectly healthy saying, "Both of your daughters are perfectly healthy, your second born just didn't want to cry."

In that instant GOD recognized the difference in the personalities of his beautiful girls. He took one last look at Jewel silently wishing she would be able to take this journey with him, but also understanding she wanted it this way, her life for her girls, a strong soldier to the end. As he stared down at Jewel she looked like she was peacefully sleeping and would awaken soon. Her skin was still the same butter cream that made his heart melt, her eyes were closed but the shape of them still drew him in. He kissed her closed lids and promised on everything, other than his girls no other woman would ever capture his heart.

The girls, who had been weighed, cleaned and swaddled, continued to rest together. One of the nurses picked them up and handed them to GOD, she was smiling and said "They are beautiful Mr. Dunbar." He looked down at mirror images of Jewel. Their skin looked like butter and their eyes were big as the moon like their mothers, but also had the diamond shape of their fathers. As GOD held both of his daughters in his arms they both woke up to look up with hazel eyes into the face of the man that would mean everything to them. It was at this moment GOD made a promise to the two most important people in his world. "The world will be yours."

GOD sat up in bed breathing heavily with his Glock at attention dripping wet from head to toe. The realization that he was once again revisiting the best and worst day of his life in the form of a nightmare made him shake his head. He put his Glock back under his silk covered pillow and got out of his California King solid mahogany bed deciding he needed a hot shower to get his mind right. It had been twenty one years since he lost his wife and it was always the same dream. GOD had always felt the dream was a way for his late wife Jewel to communicate to him something was about to go down. He welcomed the wisdom of Jewel and as he stepped into the steaming water of the shower his mind began to prepare for the worst.

Fanita Moon Pendleton

LAWRENCE "GOD" DUNBAR

The Notorious Lawrence "GOD" Dunbar was feared throughout the Hampton Roads area of Virginia as the most dangerous king pin on the east coast. But GOD's reach extends further than that to include everything from Williamsburg to the District of Columbia. Over 90% of the cocaine and heroin that invade these cities come through GOD at some point. His distribution network is strong and operates under the radar because all of his soldiers are grimy and smart; a deadly combination.

GOD and his army were also responsible for the murder rate remaining consistent in Virginia. It never fails that punks jump up to get beat down. But he was far from a street thug and didn't do shoot outs in the hood. When GOD visited, death came to his enemies and everything they loved. Entire families have been known to disappear if the Grim Reaper named GOD darkened your doorstep.

Local law enforcement always has GOD on their radar for any number of unsolved crimes, but witnesses seem to be few and far between. Not to mention the members of the criminal justice community on his payroll. GOD paid good money and used intimidation and blackmail to ensure that law enforcement stayed a safe distance away from his operation. He had police in each city as well as sheriffs, judges, lawyers, politicians and even firemen. It was a shock to everyone when a press conference was held a week after his last dream and the special prosecutor stood proudly and claimed that the infamous GOD was arrested and charged with conspiracy to commit murder and king pin drug charges.

Initially he was not worried about the charges against him; he was more pissed than anything. He found the charges to be a disruption of his day to day business operations. He had greased too many palms downtown and held too many secrets for local law enforcement to allow him to be arrested. He was seething inside and that was a sure way for death to visit someone.

His original cockiness was replaced with a reality check when he realized it wasn't local law enforcement, but the Feds who were behind his charges. Gone is any power he could hope to have in this situation. Despite his reach within local channels, GOD didn't have any specific pull over the FEDs, not even an inside man. He sat in a wing back chair in the conference room in the jail with his feet kicked up on the table, his arms folded behind his head and leaning back as if he didn't have a care in the world while he waited on his attorney Marcel Hawkins. GOD expected some answers to specific questions such as how in the hell the Feds got onto him, who in his organization was working with the Feds and how in hell are you getting me out of this?" He expected answers to these questions prior to his bond hearing or motherfuckers were gonna start dropping.

Attorney Hawkins entered the room dressed to the nines in a black wool Armani one button suit with a black pair of front lace Armani hard bottoms on his feet. He was clean and looked and smelled like money. His appearance was deceiving because he knew this meeting would not go like GOD wanted it to and he was extremely nervous.

He wiped the invisible sweat from his brow and moved towards the table placing his briefcase on the floor. The conference room was not large and the tension in the room was suffocating. GOD had yet to acknowledge his presence; he was still reclined in the chair giving Hawkins his back.

Taking a seat at the small table Hawkins cleared his throat and swallowed the lump of fear that formed into a large golf ball in his throat as he addressed GOD, "I want to apologize again for not being able to head this off at the pass." GOD's back was still turned so he continued, "The Feds are being tight lipped, they have formed a small task force and all information coming from it is on a need to know basis." With that GOD sprung from his seat and in one swift motion he had his hands wrapped around Hawkins chicken neck as he calmly growled, "You need to know." with that he released his attorney and walked out of the conference room. The deputy ran into the room, too late to make an attempt to help the attorney but in enough time to see the fear plastered on the attorney's face. The Deputy felt it was his duty to ask although he really didn't want to get involved "Are you ok Mr. Hawkins? Is there anything I can do to help?" The deputy had one hand on his gun and the other on the door handle as Hawkins shook his head, "No deputy I am fine." Hawkins picked up his briefcase and made his way past the deputy and left the conference room.

The next day GOD sat in the holding pen at the court with other inmates scheduled to hear their fate. The holding pen smelled of dirty feet and bad breath. The majority of the men waiting were black and coming before the court on drug charges. They all knew who GOD was and every last one of them stayed on their side of the room afraid to catch the wrath of GOD. When he was escorted into the courtroom GOD noticed the majority of the people in charge were white. He laughed inside thinking "I guess the justice system is black and white; the majority of defendants are black and the majority of the decision makers are white." He shook his head as he was lead to his seat at the front of the courtroom. Marcel Hawkins was standing near the prosecutor's table chopping it up with the federal prosecutor Jonathan Williams. They looked to be deep in conversation and GOD hoped for Hawkin's sake they were negotiating the charges being dropped.

GOD took time to survey the spectators in attendance and quickly nodded to a number of GOD's army seated conspicuously throughout the room. They looked like young attorneys or stock brokers decked out in their Gucci suits and appearing to be taking notes. Little did people know some where recording names of participants, others were drawing precise pictures and the remaining were writing down any important facts discussed. The twins were not in attendance. This was by design; GOD did not want too much exposure on them. In the first pew behind the defendants table sat GOD's parents Pops Dunbar and his mother Jessie Dunbar along with his Uncle Donavan and his best friend Michael.

The chatter in the courtroom was interrupted as the side door next to the witness stand opened and a bailiff entered the courtroom followed by a white man in his early fifties. He was dressed in a black robe and wearing thick Coke bottle glasses. The bailiff yelled "All rise. Hear ye, hear ye, the Federal Court for the Eastern District Court of Virginia is in session -- the Honorable Judge Allen Roberts presiding. All having business before this honorable court draw near, give attention, and you shall be heard. You may be seated." Everyone in the courtroom took their seat and attorney Williams gave the court a detailed history of alleged crimes that GOD had been accused of in the past. Attorney Hawkins objected loudly saying "Your honor the prosecutor is presenting the court with alleged offenses for which my client has never been convicted." Williams grabbed papers from the hand of one of his lackeys and waved it in the air saying "That is our point exactly your honor." Williams stopped and took a deep breath before continuing "It is The People's assertion that Lawrence 'GOD' Dunbar has never been convicted of the many crimes he has been accused of." He waved the paper in the air, "Because he has been free to make those charges disappear in the past we are asking the court to deny bail today not only because the charges against Mr. Dunbar are serious but because he has a tendency to manipulate the system to his benefit to avoid prosecution." Hawkins shot up from his seat so fast his chair fell to the ground as he screamed out "Objection Your Honor!"

GOD knew at this point he was in trouble. Gone was Hawkins normally cool exterior, he seemed anxious and easily rattled as he shouted louder than necessary, "The prosecutor is attempting to present facts not in evidence!" Williams moved forward in an attempt to gain the courts attention however Judge Roberts had heard enough.

Judge Roberts raised his frail looking hands at both attorneys and spoke "I have heard enough; this is a bond hearing, not a trial. Defendant will be remanded to the Norfolk City Jail pending trial." and with that he slammed his black gavel hard on the bench and asked the next case to be called.

Attorney Marcel Hawkins fell back into his chair and stared straight ahead, he dared not look in the direction of his client. He knew this was not good for him, but he didn't know what he could do other than offer a bone to GOD. He finally grew some balls and turned towards GOD and said "I am going to file an appeal and have bond reconsidered, right now."

GOD gave Hawkins the death grill which is normally reserved for those who are close to meeting their maker; he stood from his chair as the bailiff approached to escort him back to the holding pen he said "Get your house in order." GOD then turned to the audience and gave a slight smile to his family and quickly made eye contact with each member of his army and gave them a nod. He was quickly escorted from the room before he could see his family leave.

Many local jails are paid to house federal prisoners. The Norfolk Sheriff was pleased to have GOD in the jail because of the financial benefit to his budget. GOD was glad he was remanded to a local jail; but that happiness was short lived when the Feds had him transferred to the Northern Neck Regional Jail in Warsaw, Virginia within a week. This move was deliberate; the Feds knew the type of power GOD held in the Hampton Roads area, and they needed to limit his influence. But that's where they fucked up; by underestimating the man. They only knew GOD from what they read on paper, they were not fully versed on just how far his reach extended. This misjudgment would prove to be to their detriment.

DOMINIQUE

Dominique checked her White Mother of Pearl Rolex for the 2nd time in the last 10 minutes and thought out loud *"Where this muthafucka at?"* She was becoming impatient sitting at his crib in her champagne Range Rover, the most incognito car she owned. It was 7:00 in the morning and it was time for working people to begin moving around. The sun was peeking through the blue sky and birds were singing the same song they sing everyday around this time. The neighborhood was coming to life and she wanted to be long gone by the time families began to emerge from their over the top mansions.

The Lynnhaven River section of Virginia Beach is filled with extraordinary stone and brick custom built homes. There isn't a home in the neighborhood with a price tag less than two million. Attorney Hawkins had a 4 bedroom, 7 bathroom, 8600 square foot home nestled on 4 acres with the Lynnhaven River in its shadow. Dominique did her research as usual and she knew the entire floor plan of the home; she appreciated the exquisite details and craftsmanship of the home with its grand foyer with/cathedral ceilings, gourmet kitchen, boat dock and jet ski ramps. Thinking "Hawkins knows how to do it; too bad I got to fuck this whole spot up."

Dominique had been watching Hawkins like a hawk for a month and she knew his every move; from what time he took a shit to what time he jacked off. She followed him from his home, to work, and his after work activities. She knew where his ex-wife lived as well as where his children attended college.

Dominique left no stone unturned. She knew where he banked; how much liquid assets he held and the combination to his home safe. But she could give a fuck about all of that bullshit. Hawkins crossed GOD and that was enough to send him straight to hell and Dominique was the right woman for the job.

Attorney Hawkins normal routine was to leave home at 6:45am. It was now 7:05am and Dominique was ready to murder someone; thinking out loud she blew out *"Now on the day I am ready to rock his ass to sleep he change shit up!"* She checked her watch again and surveyed her surroundings.

Dominique felt like something was off, but she knew it wasn't her planning because her planning was impeccable. GOD always insisted on it. She let her mind drift as she wondered to a time when GOD had sat her down and gave her words of wisdom.

"Dominique you can't ever let these muthafuckas catch you out here slipping.*"*

This was one of those talks Dominique always loved so much. GOD was teaching her the game, giving her the business. GOD fixed himself a Hennessey and Coke, kicked his feet up onto his leather sectional and motioned for his daughter to sit with him. The room always smelled so good to Dominique, on this occasion it smelled like Issey Miyake and she couldn't help but get lost in the scent as she listened to her father.

Although they were relaxed GOD made sure Dominique knew this is serious business. He never wanted his seeds to be caught slipping, because this game took no prisoners man, woman or child.

With his drink in his hand he swirled the ice cubes around and looked into the eyes of his second born child...the one who refused to cry at birth...already a tough bitch he thought as he offered his teachings saying,

"You got to be methodical and plan everything out, never be in a hurry to murk a motherfucker because you will and can always get back, Your signature is your patience". The ice cubes were still moving in the glass as he brought the drink to his lips and took a swig of the caramel colored concoction.

When GOD was teaching Dominique she always gave him her undivided attention and she took everything he said as gospel. She would be soaking up information like a gangsta sponge. Like a straight A student in the front of the class wearing Coke bottle glasses; she was gonna come out on top. Out of the twins Dominique was the one who always wanted to be just like him, like the son he never had. She wanted to let him know he molded a real soldier, a true gangsta. She understood what her father was saying and she knew shit was real. This game is real and slipping was not an option; it's not what Dunbar's did.

The sound of a trash can being pushed down a driveway brought her focus back to the task at hand. She could think about her discussions with her father in the midst of being on the hunt, because it always made her mind sharper. Dominique missed having those talks with GOD, "I miss my daddy," Dominique said out loud before she even realized it came out. That's when the smile came across her face because she was about to wreck shop on everybody that fucked with her daddy. There was about to be bad blood and she planned to leave it all in the streets straight like that.

She refocused her mind on the job at hand; she had an eerie feeling she couldn't put her finger on. GOD had taught both girls to pay close attention to things that go bump in the night. Dominique began to scan the yards again before the sound of a door closing brought forth one of the objects of her obsession, "There that ho ass nigga go," she thought as she righted herself in her seat and a sinister smile crept in the corners of her mouth. Her adrenaline was pumping, this was her favorite time, the time when she was about to fuck something up.

Attorney Marcel Hawkins walked down his steps and walked towards his vehicle. He walked with the stride of a man who didn't have a care in the world. He had stopped looking over his shoulders weeks ago for the wrath of GOD; he felt like as long as GOD was locked up he couldn't touch him. He was dressed to impress with his black Armani Suit and his Gucci shoes. Hawkins was whistling and admiring his SUV as he strode towards it; he was sure he could see his reflection in the SUV.

He was sure he had the best ride out of any of his well-off neighbors and that thought alone made his smile even brighter.

Watching Hawkins' smile broaden as he walked caused a new fire to burn down her back. Dominique began to get heated speaking out loud like someone could hear her;

"Oh you big time now huh? Rocking that new Lexus LX SUV chromed out with all the perks, shit that bitch was eighty stacks easy. You still flossing off my daddy back huh.? I got you though." She regulated her breathing as she continued to watch him waiting for the exact moment to exact her father's revenge.

Dominique felt that familiar rush, the rush she got when someone was about to get split into; when someone's life was in her hands and they were at her mercy. Once the twins got the word from GOD that Hawkins had to go the planning phase had begun. Nothing the twins did was by accident or without planning. It wasn't how they were raised. GOD always told them patience is their signature and no one could fuck with that.

Hawkins had fucked up and his ass had to get it, simple as that. The twins felt there was no way he should have let their daddy be locked up. In Dominique's mind there was nothing else to talk about, "This nigga has to get dealt with."

In the last month Hawkins lost two bond hearings and failed to find the leak in GOD's army. Every time the twins saw his arrogant ass they made new plans for him to take a dirt nap. The surveillance was necessary to ensure their eventual plan was invisible. Hawkins believed he was too visible a person for anything to happen to him. Marcel Hawkins was known as the hardest working attorney in Virginia, he secretly promoted the title, but always acted annoyed by it in public. He had been on retainer for GOD for over ten years and although he was not privy to the specifics of GOD's business he has handled many criminal matters for his organization. He had made himself a small fortune off the criminal element and had developed quite an extravagant lifestyle. He had amassed a mansion in Virginia Beach, a private retreat in the Poconos and a beach house in Miami. All of his children were in college with their tuition paid in full and he could afford two mistresses and an ex-wife.

Hawkins had been able to do so well and survive because he normally through his own channels knew ahead of time about any charges that were coming down on his clients, he actually really felt blindsided by the federal governments indictment. This was intentional by the government as the number of leaks in the local criminal justice community was the main reason for the secret federal undercover sting. He knew he fucked up and would have to get creative and that meant dirty because the government does not play fair.

Dominique was so focused on Hawkins as he finally made it inside of his SUV she almost forgot about her stalker. She looked in her rear view mirror smiling to herself as she thought out loud, "Look at his ass."

Shannon Gibson, Jr. or Shadow as everyone even Dominique called him, was watching her from behind the wheel of a midnight blue Hummer that fit in with the neighborhood. He had been following Dominique for about a week now and she wasn't quite sure why. Dominique just shook her head and turned her attention back to Hawkins as he righted himself in the front seat of his SUV. Watching him made Dominique's blood boil. She needed to stay focused so she pulled up her mental rolodex to remember what her daddy used to say about emotions on a job.

GOD had a way of leaving lasting impressions on his girls, dropping wisdom all the time; he believed this would be the difference between life and death in this game. He knew he had a true gangstress in both Monique and Dominique, but they were women none the less so he was sure to discuss emotions with them. Dominique needed this talk more so than Monique, and GOD was sure to give it to her.

"Listen to me baby girl; emotions will fuck a job up. Emotions breed mistakes. I don't give a fuck what's going on, separate your emotions from the task at hand. Remember your signature, emotions and patience don't mix. You the baddest bitch but you can't be that and be emotional. Got me?"

GOD always had a way of keeping it real that brought it home for Dominique. Remembering those many lessons gave Dominique the energy to say *"Fuck Hawkins and how he rocking that shit, I'm bout to rock his ass to sleep."*

That was just about the time Hawkins started the Lexus without a care in the world. That's where he made his second mistake; his first one was fucking with GOD. His next one was thinking the twins going to check that ass....***BOOM***

The sound of Hawkins' car exploding killed the quiet of the Lynnhaven River neighborhood. Car parts went flying through the sky and the smell of burning flesh was heavy in the air. Dominique sat back in her Rover, with her thumb still on the button and a slight smile on her face.

"Don't fuck with GOD!" Dominique said out loud with a deep bitterness that came from the depths of her soul as she quietly pulled out of the chaotic neighborhood. She watched in her rearview as people spilled into their yards in an attempt to witness the destruction first hand. As she glided out of the neighborhood she was smiling deep down inside of her soul.

Shadow was still in the cut watching with a mix of amazement and lust

"DAMNNNNN Dominique fucked his ass up fo sho!" Debris was everywhere and Shadow was hyped from watching the sleepy neighborhood get all the way turned up. "I think I'm in love, this chick is made for me for real," he said as he started his truck and quietly followed Dominique out of the neighborhood, getting lost in all the chaos.

Shadow was a gunslinger, always had been, he got that honest from his pops. He played for keeps and didn't take shit from nobody. He has known the twins since they were all kids.

"Shit I have wanted to fuck Dominique since I knew what pussy was," Shadow thought as he kept watching the flames grow as he exited the neighborhood. "I bet I could have her, but her so called nigga Jamal is blocking a nigga flow."

As he followed Dominique out of the neighborhood, Shadow's mind drifted back to a recent altercation with Jamal at one of his pops Killer Kuts barbershop spots.

Killer Kut's was hopping with activity as usual when Shadow entered. The stereo was blasting the latest by Jay Z and Shadow noticed a couple of his friends shooting dice in one corner of the shop. As he continued to scan the room, he noticed that bitch ass nigga Jamal and just shook his head.

Shadow knew who Jamal was; he had seen him hugged up with Dominique a couple of times which made his blood boil more than it should have. Shadow thought to himself, "I don't know why I am pissed off, she not my woman." But his heart wouldn't let him finish this thought without adding, yet to that statement, "She not my woman yet." Before he knew it the word "Damn" flew out of his mouth loud enough to make others in the shop take notice. He noticed Jamal look his way and then attempt to play it off. Jamal was sitting in the barber chair chopping it up with a group of old heads while getting a tight edge up by one of the best barbers in town when he noticed Shadow glaring at him.

Jamal's barber Curt who was hooking Jamal's cut up looked up from his station where he was working his usual magic and asked, "What's good Shadow dog, what you over there talking about?" Curt was a big brother; 6'5 and about 260 pounds of solid muscle. He was fair skinned with wavy hair which he kept cut short. Shadow grew up with Curt, he was the ladies-man, and Shadow hung around him because all the flyest bitches flocked to this nigga by the car load. They had always been cool.

Shadow looked at his stick man ignoring the heated looks he was getting from Jamal and said, "I'm good Curt, what's good wit cha?"

Curt oblivious to the heat that was building up between his good friend and one of his regular customers stopped hooking Jamal's head up again and said "Shadow help a brotha out. I'm trying to talk Jamal here into hooking me up with Monique fine ass.

I mean shit he fucking Dominique, but he won't hook a nigga up, now how foul is that?" They erupted into laughter as someone yelled out "That's too much woman for your Curt!" and the room dissolved into laughter once again.

The heat in Shadow's face didn't go unnoticed by those who could see him, especially Jamal. Shadow was unable to place where the heat was coming from but he was ready to erupt. Being that nigga, Jamal knew it was time to get on his gangsta. He recognized a look in Shadow's eyes; the look said it was about to be some shit; but Jamal couldn't place the beef. He scanned the room and spotted the two patrons who were posing as customers. They were actually members of GOD's army so he knew his back was straight.

He returned his glare to Shadow. He couldn't figure out was why this fool was looking so pissed, thinking, "He must be feeling one of the twins, but hell which one cause Dominique is sho off limits. Hell if Marcus Monique's bodyguard had anything to say about it so is Monique." Jamal kept his guard up and his ice grill straight on Shadow.

As Shadow stood in the center of the shop he absorbed the looks sent his way from a couple of people. He couldn't control what was happening to him and lord knows he wanted to, but his mouth was speaking louder than his brain and before Shadow could stop himself he blurted out,

"Dominique is not fucking this busta ass nigga," he motioned towards Curt's station pointing directly at Jamal and continued, and only a bitch would be in here telling lies like that!" A collective hush came over the whole shop. Real niggas knew some shit was about to go down and they waited with hood anticipation to see how it was going to be handled.

Although Jamal was strapped and had his boys with him, he did recognize this was Shadow's pops Rolla's place and most likely Rolla already had a weapon trained on his ass anticipating some shit. So Jamal the strategist just shook his head from side to side, grilled Shadow and said "I appreciate you trying to defend Dom's honor, but if you know anything about her, you know she can handle her own. As for that other shit you said, it's obvious you not ready to play in my league so go on upstairs with your pops and get schooled some more, and then step to a grown man the right way."

There were hushed chuckles heard throughout the shop. But all attention was on the two men engaged in a Texas standoff of stares. The stereo that was now bumping the latest by 2Chainz mysteriously lost some of its sound and the other barbers took breaks from their duties to ensure they wouldn't miss any of the excitement. The guys getting their hair cut didn't have any complaints. That's how it is in the hood, motherfuckers were always down to see an Ali vs. Frazier confrontation. And they gave their full attention to the center of the ring.

The look of embarrassment on Shadow's face was enough to make muthafuckas clown, but they knew it would be like a death sentence up in the spot, so they said nothing. What they couldn't understand was he wasn't embarrassed because of the bitch shit Jamal said; but more so because he didn't want niggas knowing he was feeling Dominique that deep. Shadow was contemplating letting the shit slide, but the devil on his back refused to let the shit go.

Curt was dusting Jamal's head off and removing his cape holding his own head down in silence, feeling like he had sparked shit off but there was no way he could of known what Shadow and Jamal both were feeling when it came to Dominique.

Jamal paid Curt and then he and his boys got ready to bounce, but not before Jamal dug into Shadow one more time. The tension in the air was thick as Jamal stepped square in Shadow's face, removing all personal space and spoke words for Shadow's ears only, "That pussy is wet, tight, and its mine....don't get fucked up!"

As Jamal turned to leave Shadow grabbed him from behind placing him in a sleeper hold, Jamal's boys attempted to make a move towards Shadow but were met with a barricade of Mac 10's coming from what were assumed to have been patrons awaiting haircuts. Every weapon in the spot was trained on Jamal's boys daring them to make a move. They wisely slowed their roll. It could get real fucked up, real quick.

Shadow knew his back was protected so he bent concentrated on the task at hand as he whispered into Jamal's ear for only him to hear, "I am not the one to fuck wit. I will destroy your world and everyone in it, don't' you get fucked up!" After speaking those words Shadow put Jamal to sleep with the precision of a trained assassin.

He let Jamal's body drop to the floor and turned his attention to the boys with him and said "The only reason any of you will leave here today alive is because of GOD, stay the fuck out of my way." With that Shadow turned and made eye contact with the occupants of the shop and gave each of them a head nod and they began to lower their weapons. Jamal's boys scooped him up and headed out of the shop. Shadow was pissed and decided he was going to make both Jamal and Dominique pay for playing him for a punk.

Shadow could hear the sirens in the distance as he made a smooth and unnoticed exit from the neighborhood. He understood Dominique was a female gangstress, harder than most men he knew. But what most bitches and bitch ass niggas didn't know is Shadow was a true killer. He tried to never mix business with pleasure and would put in work at the drop of a hat.

Shadow's main problem and the reason he was not on the same level with Dominique is because he had not been schooled in the art of the game. Sure he was an excellent shot; and his murder game was on point, he got that honest from his pops, but because he never had a mentor like GOD or paid attention to that side of the life his pops tried to school him on, he failed to understand the planning and patience it takes to pull a plan together. Shadow knew where the weakness in his game was and with his latest assignment of killing Dominique he decided to try things differently. She was making him break his business with pleasure rule. "I only agreed to fuck with this job because I could destroy Dominique and Jamal."

Shadow had been following Dominique for a week; he peeped the shit she was doing with the attorney and decided to let her get her shit off thinking, "Some people need killing, and one less lawyer is not going to hurt nothing." He wondered why the twin's uncle Dollar Bill wanted to kill them so bad. "I don't understand why he just don't bum rush they pretty asses and take over their operation, they some tough bitches no doubt but he a Dunbar too; surely he has ways to get them to see things his way; I mean they are his nieces." Shadow adjusted his rearview mirror and continued following behind Dominique as his brain, heart, and dick where doing the tango trying to reconcile his personal feelings. He was feeling something strange inside, something he didn't want to understand, but he did and thought *"Fuck."*

Dominique took a quick look in the side mirror as she drove down Military Highway and laughed, she saw Shadow was still following her and just shook her head thinking "I been on to his ass from almost the first day he began following me but decided to continue to play it off so I could watch his dumb ass." She continued cruising trying to decide if she wanted to ditch Shadow or let him tag along. Dominique wanted to go to her low key crib in the Popular Halls section of Norfolk because she was in need of some good sleep, but she had a stop to make first and decided to let Shadow tag alone thinking, "Yeah I'ma let him follow me as a reminder shit can get real bad...real fast."

LOCKDOWN

Breaking news….. *"I am standing outside of the Virginia Beach home of renowned attorney Marcel Hawkins where there has been what appears to be a bombing. It has not yet been confirmed if attorney Hawkins was in the vehicle that was bombed, but things do not look hopeful."*

GOD watched the KJND news broadcast as the pretty white lady brought him the best news he had heard all day. The TV showed the destruction of the expensive landscaping and the chaos of fire trucks and ambulances as the news media attempted to bring the tragedy into everyone's living room. GOD's smile broadened and he shook his head up and down with his arms folded across his chest. He knew his baby girl was speaking to him through the walls of Northern Neck Regional Jail. Sitting in the dayroom starring at the old black and white 19 inch TV GOD knew damn well Hawkins was in that car when it blew him to hell. His baby girl's signature was all over it. The smile on the inside of GOD's soul was too much. He knew once he gave the order Dominique wouldn't let that shit go. No one got away with fucking with her daddy, *"Naw my baby girl going to put something hot to all they ass and they won't ever know it's coming,"* he thought. GOD shook his head up and down and continued to smile deep down inside because he knew there would not be any trace of her ever being there. She was too well trained. He leaned back in his chair and reflected on how well his seeds had learned their lessons.

"Girls today is your 6th birthday and it's time for you ladies to learn something new." Today his girls would begin their long journey to being the baddest bitches around. GOD looked at two sets of eyes that were already large get larger with anticipation. Those eyes that stared back at him, the eyes of his twin girls Monique and Dominique made him feel as if he could connect with Jewel directly. Through them he saw her.

Some might not agree with what he was about to do. Some might think his girls should be sitting around playing with a white fucking Barbie doll or coloring in a fucking coloring book, but GOD knew his girls had to learn everything about the game, everything about getting to the money and commanding power and respect.

"Daddy what are we going to learn?"

That's Dominique; always down for whatever. She was the more inquisitive of the two. eager to learn, but never trying to impress. Monique was the thinker of the two, she was down like four flat tires, but even at 6 played life like a chess game with no sudden movements.

With the two most important people in his life flanking him, GOD grabbed them both by the hand and spoke in the serious tone they recognized, "You will begin your hand to hand combat and your weapons training. I want you two to listen and absorb everything, embrace it, feel it in your bones and over the next 6 years you will become the best."

Both girls had heard their daddy talk about this since they were 5 and couldn't believe the time was actually here. When they were alone they talked about it non-stop vowing to help each other do their best. They both wanted to please their father and at 5 and 6 years old their exposure to this life had already transformed their minds and now their body and skills transformation would begin.

They both showed brilliant smiles as their father talked to them about who their personal karate trainer would be. GOD explained to them he would personally handle their weapons training.

Over the next 6 years the girls trained in the art of Karate, Tae Kwon Do, boxing, and Capoeira. They got an education on the history of weapons and by the age of 12 could handle a Glock as well as any adult member of GOD's army. They were skilled in death, but trained in precision and patience. GOD looked at his girls, they were so removed from tea parties and slumber parties, but they were still the prettiest girls he had ever seen and now they were both pretty and dangerous, just like he wanted them to be.

The KJND newscaster began to speak again, or maybe she never stopped, GOD had just zoned out for a minute *"It has been confirmed that the remains of Marcel Hawkins have been identified in the burnt vehicle."*

They dayroom had begun to fill up with other inmates who were pointing and staring at the news broadcast. Some were even clapping and shouting "Fuck all lawyers, fuck em!" over and over again.

The room was live with activity as GOD chuckled and thought to himself, *"I could have told y'all motherfuckers his ass was blown the fuck up, and believe me this is not the end. My baby girl is going to find out who the fuck been running they motherfucking mouth and then they ain't going to have no mouth to run, simple as that."*

GOD watched a group of inmates begin to set up for a game of spades or bid wiz, whichever was on tap today and began to do a mental checklist of the list of people who had to die. Hawkins made the short list and so had the woman who seemed to want him incarcerated so badly, Special Agent Lucinda Beverly. He couldn't put his finger on what was so familiar about her, but he could feel her hatred for him. The shit was funny to GOD as he thought "Her little pretty ass was really hot to lock me down, what the fuck up with her? Don't matter though, whatever it is she has earned a spot at the top of the hit list." Before he could finish putting the list together in his head the crackle of the overhead speakers intruded into the already chaotic atmosphere. "Dunbar" GOD heard his name being yelled over the loud speaker and wondered who the fuck was calling him Dunbar, they knew the rules. GOD looked up and spotted a tall lanky deputy standing near the intercom looking like his feet hurt. GOD recognized him as Deputy Drew, he had just recently been transferred to this unit. GOD gave him the side eye because he had the nerve to call him by his last name. The dayroom got extremely tense very fast, every inmate knew the deputy had fucked up and they were anxious to see him get fucked up. Any action out of the ordinary would make their day.

But for someone to cross the infamous GOD, this was something all of them would pay to see up close and personal.

Deputy Drew recalled getting the run down on all of the inmates when he transferred over but special concern was paid to Lawrence "GOD" Dunbar. Drew was told he was to be called GOD and he was never to be searched or refused special privileges. Drew wasn't trying to hear all that bullshit. He was the law and Dunbar was the inmate and that's what it was. Drew planned to show "GOD" today he was no more than an inmate, just like all of the others; no more no less.

GOD has always been a smooth nigga, smart, but deadly. He wasn't the type you would see coming and before you knew what hit you, your entire family was wiped out; they were a figment of people's imagination. One day they were there and the next …well, that's how he got down. He slowly got up from his seat and made his way to the deputy. Every eye in the room was on him with excited anticipation. Niggas love some gangsta shit. As he moved towards the intercom station GOD could see the deputy's intent was to stand his ground. His body language was too straight. There were other deputies near and GOD made eye contact with them and they began to retreat from the area, leaving their man a sitting duck. The entire sheriff's staff called him GOD and this new muthafucka wouldn't be any different.

Deputy Drew noticed the other deputies exit the dayroom and he began to question his decision to fuck with this particular inmate.

Maybe he should have just left everything as it was; who was he to come to a unit and try and change things? The deputy noticed the other inmates had stopped playing their games and many of them were sitting on tables and standing on chairs. All of them had their eyes trained on him. He became visibly shaken as GOD approached but tried hard to maintain his authoritative demeanor. GOD's demeanor on the outside was cool and calm; he approached the deputy in an almost non-threatening manner. It actually eased some of the deputy's anxiety and he was just about to relax when a quick flash like a shadow passed in front of his eyes and struck his throat. He stumbled back and fell to one knee with his hands grabbing and grasping his throat the source of his pain. He wondered what happened but the wonder was short lived when GOD bent down next to him and said "The next time you open your mouth to address me you address me as "GOD" or you might not make it home to the wife and new baby feel me?" The venom in his voice was a far cry from the display on his face or his body language. This is a man you would never see coming until it was too late.

Deputy Drew slowly got up from the concrete floor and scanned the room as other inmates were glaring at him as though they also wanted a crack at him. His throat was tight and sore but he would live. He righted himself and wanted to go into attack mode, but what could he do, he was outnumbered by the inmates. He couldn't believe his fellow deputies had put him in this situation. Deputy Drew was a hot head but the threat GOD made towards his family would keep him in line. He refused to let this job jeopardize his family.

GOD could see the struggle Deputy Drew was having with his own conscious. He hoped he made the right decision, but fuck it, if he didn't then he had to go and so did that wife and kid. GOD stuck his hands out to allow Deputy Drew to handcuff him while continuing to stare hard into his eyes. Drew began to sweat and at that moment decided to be smart for once and not think with his ego so he cleared his throat to try and get rid of the uneasiness that had settled in the pit of his stomach. . Deputy Drew felt different now; he felt it was time to go with the flow before somebody got hurt.

"GOD you have a visitor"

It was apparent the deputy had made his decision and GOD was pleased with his choice. The inmates watching the power move just shook their heads and went back to their games and shit talking.

GOD figured it must be an attorney visit because his regular visitation day was Friday which was 3 days away. He exited the day room with Deputy Drew and headed towards the visitation area.

The twins hooked GOD up with Tonya Green and Associates. Attorney Tonya Green decided to handle GOD's case personally even though she was the managing partner and normally left the grit and the grime for her associates. Green was persuaded to make an exception by one of her college sorority sisters Monique Dunbar. What Monique didn't know was Tonya would have done it without the persuasion. GOD smiled at the thought of seeing Tonya's fine ass again.

"Shit Tonya ass is fine as hell and her ass always screams to be released from those tight ass business suits. She know what she be doing. She has wanted to fuck me for years, ever since I dropped the twins off at Hampton University when she was in her last year of law school. Truth be told, I have feelings for Tonya but I was not ready to give in to them. It was easy to avoid the feelings when I was on the streets because I could immerse myself in other things. I always feel like I am disrespecting Jewel when I think about being with Tonya." These thoughts ran through GOD's mind as he was being escorted to a visitation room.

Upon entering the attorney visiting room, GOD's cuffs were removed and he gave Deputy Drew on icy glare before he exited the room. The room smelled stale, kind of like when rain first hits the cement. There wasn't any natural light coming into the room, no windows to look out and see freedom staring back at you. There was a table and two chairs, nothing more, and even they were depressing. The chairs were bolted to the floor and couldn't be moved. The table was solid steel and so heavy it couldn't be moved without the assistance of at least four able bodied men. When GOD stepped forward, he noticed something different about Tonya. She was standing with her back to him so he couldn't see her face but the stature before him was so familiar, and that smell, he would know that smell anywhere. It was the smell of White Diamonds. But it couldn't be…

"Dominique?"

Dominique turned around slowly and looked in the eyes of the only man in her life that had never let her down. She looked in the eyes of the man who taught her not only how to do her hair, put fly gear together and shoot a gun, but how to carry herself like a lady and a deadly cobra all at the same time. This man taught her how to make niggas respect her swagger despite her gender. She smiled at her father and said, "Hi Daddy. I want to run and hug you so bad!" Dominique knew she couldn't do that because right now she was posing as one of the associates at Tonya Green's firm who had come to go over an enormous amount of paperwork with GOD. She had disguised herself and actually looked like an attorney. GOD had the deputies on the unit in line; however he didn't have control of the visitation room yet.

"You can call me attorney Carmen Jones," Dominique said with a little smirk. "Monique and I really need to see you together, but that's not going to happen so with this cover we will come separately." Dominique approached the large table and had a seat and motioned for him to do the same.

As he took his seat GOD sat back and looked at his second born, he couldn't be more proud if he had put this shit together himself. Dominique began to pull fake legal forms out of her Dolce briefcase before she looked in her father's eyes and began to speak.

"Daddy... I know you heard already."

GOD knew exactly what she was talking about and began to nod his head affirmatively

"Yeah baby I did....you still dat bitch!"

Hearing that from her daddy made the little girl in Dominique smile. GOD leaned forward in his chair and gave Dominique that look, the one where she knew what he was about to say was serious. He was focused on the instructions he wanted the twins to follow.

"Listen to this shit I'm about to spit at you right now, listen like you have never done before, because the life of you and your sister is gonna depend on how well you plan out specific shit. Somebody is about to come at y'all strong."

Dominique gave her father that signature menacing smile she had when she was thinking about murking someone and said "They have no idea who they fucking with if they think Mo and I are gonna just bitch up without flat lining the whole city!"

GOD laughed out loud at his daughter's statement because he knew the twins were deadly and even though his army also knew it, many people were unaware they had been running the day to day operations behind the scenes since they were 17. He wanted them to sit down with Marcus, the head of the army's Hit Squad, and plan a series of surprises for whoever made the choice to come for the crown.

GOD trusted Marcus, he was not only Monique's personal body guard, he was in love with his Monique and there is no greater motivation than for a man to protect his own. GOD knew it was somebody close, so it would be tricky. He reminded Dominique to tighten up her circle. GOD noticed the legal pad sitting on the table and scribbled a name on it. He passed the pad to her with the name of the agent to his daughter; he knew she would know what to do with it. "They believe since I'm on lock you guys are now weak." They shared a knowing smirk and she put the pad back into her briefcase, giving her father a quick nod.

Dominique knew the next move she and Monique made would have to make a statement. Staring around the gloomy room with its sterile atmosphere only made her more determined to fuck shit up. She thought she might have a starting point as she remembered her stalker. She couldn't think of another reason for Shadow to be following her other than he was trying to find his opportunity to take over business or he was working for whoever was actually was trying to take over; it was too much of a coincidence.

She figured she would run it past her dad and get his take on it so she took her focus off the depressiveness of the room and returned it to her father saying, "I think I got a read on this shit Daddy because I got a shadow following me. Shit his name is Shadow. You might even remember him he grew up out our way in Huntersville. Shannon Gibson, Big Rolla's son."

GOD sat up close to the table and placed his hands in full view. He knew who she was talking about and smiled as he remembered the happy go lucky kid. GOD began to shake his head his smile fading and his mind working overtime, "I know Rolla don't know nothing about this. Rolla raised Shannon right, taught him how to murk niggas at an early age, Shannon is smart, he is far from stupid...somebody is selling him a blank check." GOD continued to ponder how he wanted Dominique to proceed. He knew he had to be clear because his daughter would put Shannon, or Shadow, whatever the fuck he was calling himself, to sleep without another thought about it. But GOD wanted to go a different route, Shannon was Big Rolla's son and GOD and Big Rolla went way back. Further back than anyone knew. They were very close but didn't advertise their relationship. GOD would not give the green light on eliminating his son unless it was absolutely necessary. He felt like he owed Rolla that much.

Dominique knew her father well; she could tell when something wasn't sitting right with him. She assumed he wanted her to take Shadow out as soon as possible and she knew she would have to get to the bottom of this quickly. There had to be a reason Shadow has been following her for a week. She knew he had a crush on her, he always had, and truthfully, she was kind of feeling his stupid ass too but that couldn't be why he was on her tail like this.

Dominique told her dad Shadow had followed her all the way to the jail and didn't know his tail is busted. Her plan was to make the situation work for her. GOD smiled at his youngest daughter and agreed she should not let Shadow know he fucked up but also decided he would contact his best friend Michael so he could get word to Big Rolla that he needed him to come to the jail. Thinking to himself, "If Rolla wants to save his son's life he needs to reel him in before I unleash Dominique on his ass."

Dominique really took a good look into her daddy's eyes; he was just as sharp as ever and even though he was wearing prison orange he still looked like he was rocking some silk Sean Jean shit. GOD's stature is still boss and being locked up couldn't change that. GOD was standing 6'4 with an athletic build and muscles that would make the world's strongest man cry like a bitch. His skin was the color of a black cobra, smooth and sleek like Tyrese Gibson. The bedroom diamond hazel eyes have had many of women making a damn fool of themselves over the years.

Monique and Dominique never knew their daddy to be serious about any particular women besides their mother's memory. Don't get it twisted GOD had plenty of women he put the dick to, but nobody was ever close to wifey material. That part of GOD's heart died with Jewel leaving room only for his baby girls. GOD would always say, "*All these trick ass bitches can get is some good dick.*" Dominique smiled as she thought he must be breaking they back cause they always making a damn fool of themselves to get his attention.

The loud sound of keys turning in the door signaled they needed to bring this meeting to a close. As soon as Deputy Drew stepped in Dominique went back into her role as his attorney.

"Ok Mr. Dunbar I think we have covered some solid ground. I will be back later in the week to update you on our progress and make any adjustments."

The look in GOD's eyes could only be described as pride in its purest form. GOD thought about the vision before him; from their mother his girls got their beautiful looks, body and spirit. From GOD his beautiful girls got their hustle, their instincts, and their gangsta. He couldn't have asked for anything better.

GOD told Ms. Jones he looked forward to hearing from her just as Deputy Drew handcuffed him but not before he addressed him as GOD. He laughed on the inside but gave Drew the death stare that said it all "*Take me to my shit.*"

Back in his single man cell GOD noticed the unit was still turned up as he began to reflect on Jewel and the tragic life she led before he made her his woman. He thought about a night early in their budding relationship when Jewel shared her childhood memory of how she first came to live in the neighborhood.

Jewel's parents were both junkies, they showed up one morning in 1971 with Jewel for a visit at her grandparents. Jewel thought Grandma Mary Lee was a beautiful woman; 8-year old Jewel couldn't keep her eyes off of her.

*G-Ma, as a young Jewel called her grandmother, had
skin that reminded Jewel of the caramel inside of her
favorite candy, the one she only got on special occasions.
G-Ma was about 5'7 with what black folk in the 70's
called good hair and a shape that men in the 70's called
brick house bad. It was rumored Grandpa Lee had to
bust a couple of heads over G-Ma Lee.*

*Jewel described her Grandma Mary as a strong
willed woman who knew her daughter and son-in-law
were in trouble and it would only get worse. Jewels
parents weren't just smoking weed, no they were fucking
with heroin or boy as it was called on the streets. Heroin
had a way of taking over your body, and soul. Jewel was
visibly shaken as she recalled for GOD that Grandma
Mary helplessly watched as her daughter disintegrated
into the world of lost souls. There was no point in
arguing with Jewel's mother, the drugs were too
powerful. Both of her grandparents decided to put their
foot down and take their grandbaby regardless of if
Jewel's mother and father liked it or not.*

*Jewel recalled her grandmother promised she
wouldn't allow her daughter to drag the only grandbaby
she had through the streets any longer. She remembered
her grandmother hugging her and then yelling at her
mother that her precious granddaughter had not been fed
properly in days and that for 8 years old she was clearly
underweight.*

Jewel, who took after her grandmother with and had beautiful shoulder length silky hair that was matted to her head. The clothes that Jewel wore were so dirty that it was hard for her grandmother to make out the original color.

She got choked up as she remembered her grandmother went to the kitchen to fix her grandbaby a plate of the roast, macaroni and cheese, collards and cornbread she had just finished making. When Grandma Mary called out to Jewel to come and eat she got no answer.

Jewel heard her grandmother, but she could not answer her. After calling her again and getting no answer Jewel saw Grandma Mary come into the room where she found Jewel on the floor by the front door with her head bowed to her knees crying softly.

She knew her parents had left her and they were not coming back. As her Grandmother held her close to her breast Jewel heard her say her parents did what was best for her because their lifestyle would have surely killed any spirit Jewel could have hoped to develop.

For years Jewel would sit on the porch and stare up and down the street hoping her parents would come back for her, but they never did. Throughout Jewels childhood she would hear rumors about her parents, rumors about their drug use and their criminal activities. Kids being the mean hearted people they are would tease Jewel, telling her she didn't have a momma.

The pain Jewel experienced from the absence of her parents went deep. For years she felt inadequate, as if she was not enough. Jewel felt the important people in her life would always leave her. These feelings were deep and although G-Ma tried, she was never able to take that sadness away from Jewel.

GOD realized he had dozed off as he remembered the story his beloved Jewel told him. He recalled telling her he would never leave her. That is one of the reasons he had never let another woman fill the part of his heart Jewel occupied. Women just assumed he was a user, even though he spoiled them they were never able to touch his life like they wanted to. There was only one woman that had come close and that was Tonya Green, which is why he avoided her. GOD knew after twenty-one years, Jewel would prefer for him to be happy but he wasn't sure how to let go.

GO GETTERS

Monique was sometimes known as the deadliest twin. She was the one that moved in silence. Her beauty was unparalleled; well there was one other that could hold a candle to her and that was her twin. The bond between the twins was built on love, trust and loyalty. They were best friends and shared everything, including their first kill when they turned 17. They had to strategize and decide what the best course of action would be. Sitting behind her desk in her home office Monique thought back on the days leading up to the hit.

Stealing from GOD is just as bad as snitching. Kashawn or Kilo as he was known on the street was a supervisor in one of GOD's dope spots located on B Ave in the Huntersville section of Norfolk. This is where the dope was cooked up. Kilo was responsible for making sure the dope was right and keeping the girls in line. The dope was coming up short at Kilo's spot. GOD didn't confront Kilo. He never believed in asking a question he didn't already know the answer to. So until he found out who was stealing from him, he decided to sit back in the cut and watch his operation from the outside looking in.

Sunday was the only day the cook house was closed down. GOD had his dude Jamal, a dangerous man in his own right, install surveillance equipment throughout the spot. GOD and the twins spent time watching everyone who entered and exited the premises. They noticed a woman leaving the cook house, the body on her would make anyone pay attention. Her curves were hypnotic, thick in all the right places with a booty you could sit several glasses on.

But that's not what caught their eye. What they saw was how she looked over her shoulder and fumbled around in her purse and that's when they saw it. She took out a large paper bag and kissed it. GOD wondered to himself, "What do we have here?"

Dominique was driving a burgundy minivan GOD borrowed from one of his cousins and they followed this woman for 10 more blocks. She stopped on the corner of Church Street and Princess Anne Rd. Monique broke the silence by wondering out loud,

"Who the hell is she waiting for?"

The question was answered in an instant as Kilo pulled up to the corner in his burnt orange two tone Range Rover bumping Biggie and leaning out the window. The girl hopped in and leaned over and kissed Kilo sloppily on the mouth.

"I'll be damned," they all said.

"His ass gots to go!" was the only response GOD gave.

It was the only response the twins needed to hear. Monique and Dominique followed Kilo for a week and decided the best way to get to him without disrupting business but also make an example out of him and his little bitch was to get them when they were together in his home. The method they choose to use would be extremely gruesome.

The twins were pissed. Dominique, the more vocal of the two was gritting her teeth so hard Monique was afraid she would break one. Her anger boiled over as she yelled out,

"Muthefuckas got to know you can't steal from GOD. My Daddy is the reason muthafuckas is eating on a regular; this shit will not be tolerated!"

Monique watched her sister get louder with her rants and just shook her head because she knew when Dominique was like this, somebody somewhere was about to get it. Dominique got her knife set out. She was deadly with the right weapon in her hand and took pleasure in completing any task given.

It was after one in the morning when the twins pulled up to the Crown Pointe Townhomes in Norfolk. It was easy to find as they had followed Kilo so many times. Crown Pointe was a pretty decent neighborhood and at this time of morning the neighborhood was asleep. In Kilo's house there was a light on upstairs but the rest of the house was dark.

Monique was the best at picking locks so she took on that task. Both girls had stealth abilities and could enter the home without being detected. They were both wearing black cat suits with all black DC's. Dominique checked her knapsack one last time and slipped on her gloves. The light illuminating from upstairs actually gave the twins all the light they needed.

It didn't take Monique long to gain entrance to the home and the twins headed straight for the steps leading to the lighted bedroom. The sounds coming from upstairs became louder as the twins approached the room. You could hear the headboard banging against the wall and Kilo talking shit like he was king ding-a-ling. But the moans coming from the girl were muffled like she was being suffocated, she was barely audible.

Monique slowly pushed the door open and they could now clearly see what was happening. Kilo had duct tape over the girl's mouth and her hands tied behind her back. Kilo had his hands squarely around the girl's neck and his 10 inch dick pushed to the hilt in her ass. He was banging her so hard he didn't even notice their presence in the room. It wasn't until Dominique yanked him around his neck with a wire so thick it damn near severed his neck from his shoulders he realized his home had been invaded.

The pain in his neck was beyond excruciating but despite the pain he could see who had come for him. Dressed in black cat suits and standing five foot eleven he knew he wasn't seeing double, he knew who stood before him. It was GOD's seeds. They had come for him. He knew he had to pay. But not like this. He couldn't go out like this. Kilo decided to lunge for Dominique; she appeared to be the one in control and that's where he fucked up.

Fanita Moon Pendleton

When Kilo, holding his neck jumped towards Dominique, Monique came off the top rope on his ass with a body blow that would have made Stone Cold Steve Austin proud. He hit the floor so hard his head bounced off the hard wood floor. The twins were on him before he could breathe. A foot to the neck held him still and his arms were duct tapped and then his legs. Kilo was placed in a seated position on a couch in the sitting area of the room.

The sound of something hitting the floor hard caught the girl's attention. It was the girl from the bed; she had rocked back and forth until she made herself fall. Dominique called her a stupid ass as she grabbed her to join the party.

Kilo looked into the eyes of the assassins GOD had sent for him, yes he called them assassins. He knew they were girls, but they were putting the murder game down straight like that. Kilo began to berate himself for taking GOD's dope.

"Fuck, why did I fuck with GOD's dope? I didn't really need it. I was eating, I just wanted more. And look what it has got me."

Monique moved towards the couch as she watched Kilo making attempts to free himself. If it wasn't so serious it would be comical. Shaking her head she said, "Kilo you already know what it is. You are about to be a walking advertisement for GOD.

You are about to show everybody else what happens when you cross GOD." With that Monique chopped off Kilo's right hand and Dominique chopped off his left.

The screams that came from the room were drowned out by the music coming from the surround sound Dominique had turned up. An old cut by Lil Kim was playing "Queen Bitch.".

"Ha-ha yes, that shit is right on time, because this nigga sure has run into the Queen Bitches for real."

Monique decided to take things a step further and cut Kilo's big dick off, just the sight made the girl cry even harder. Monique moved like a panther towards the chick and put the knife to her throat, "Bitch I swear, if you don't shut the fuck up." Monique looked over her shoulder and called her sister "Yo Dom come shut this ho up."

Dominique moved towards the grief stricken girl and took her .38 caliber pistol with the silencer attached and shot the girl dead center. She was dead before another thought could cross her mind.

Monique stuck Kilo's dick in the girls mouth and said "Suck on this bitch, you should watch the company ya keep."

Kilo's head was severed from his body and placed on the bed with his hands. The twins turned the music down and began to search the home. The product was long gone but there was over a million dollars in cash in the home. The twins took that and left the home locking the front door on their way out.

An anonymous call was made to the Norfolk Police Department within the hour.

Back at his crib GOD watched the newscast of the tragedy in Crown Point with the rest of his army. He called an impromptu meeting of all his soldiers at his meeting house. This is not the home where he laid his head; this is where he held family business meetings and gatherings. Everyone was in front of the 70 inch screen wondering who had the balls to go up against GOD. Many agreed Kilo was a real nigga that couldn't be taken out easily. They all had drinks in their hands and were eating light snacks when in walked the twins.

The newscast ended and GOD's army was getting louder and vowing to find out what the fuck was going on. Monique and Dominique dressed exquisitely from head to toe took center stage. They both had on black Lela Rose mini dresses fit their bodies to perfection. Giuseppe Stiletto pumps, Dior glasses and oversized hand bags added the finesse to the look, but their hair pulled up off of their face showing their long necks and butter skin made every man in the room forget what the topic of conversation had just been.

The twins knew the effect they had on men, they stood 5'11 with 130 well placed pounds. Some people call them redbone but GOD told them they had their mothers skin; like butter pecan. Both girls had an athletic body from all their training. The thickness of their thighs and the tightness of their stomachs were a testament to the many workouts they still endured.

The three things that caught most men's eye were the 36C firm breasts, the raindrop asses that stood up at attention begging to be rubbed, and their diamond shaped eyes. Men thought they were either a cross between Sanai Lathan and Beyonce or just fine as shit. They wore their jet black hair exactly the same length and you wouldn't be able to tell them apart unless you knew them. GOD had schooled them on how to use it to their advantage when necessary. And if they chose to give their heart to a man he had to be on their level or above.

Monique and Dominique stepped into the sunken living room and stood on opposite sides of GOD who was seated. GOD turned the TV down and commanded the attention of his soldiers. As he began to address the room, the men began to look from GOD, to Monique, to Dominique.

GOD addressed his soldiers "Kilo was stealing from the family, he was taking away from your table and how you feed your family. There is no room in this family for disloyalty, stealing or snitching. Any instance of it will be dealt with swiftly. What you have witnessed tonight is Monique and Dominique putting their murder game down."

The murmurs in the room got so loud GOD had to stand up to regain control. Jamal, a rising star in GOD's army stood up and asked GOD to clarify his statement. GOD looked at the twins and nodded his head. Monique, the more communicative of the two began to speak. Her tone was feminine but authoritative.

When she spoke she demanded attention without being loud and boisterous.

"Dominique and I canceled Kilo and the bitch he had helping him steal from the family. There was no product left in the home but we did recover cash."

The twins reached into their oversized Dior hand bags and pulled out envelops already labeled with each person's name on it. Each envelope contained twenty thousand in cash.

Monique continued, "Everyone will eat but deception will not be tolerated. Does anyone have anything they want to add?"

Everyone looked from Monique, to GOD, to Dominique and they could tell by the look in their eyes the torch had been passed. Some didn't know how they felt about it, but after what they saw today they knew the girls had a tight ass murder game. They would wait and see if they could continue to get this money. Well almost everyone. From the back of the room he stood there heated, pissed off that decisions were being made without him, as if he didn't exist. In his mind he began to think about all the money he had made for this family, all the death he had handed down in the name of this family and thought,

"I am going to get passed over for these pretty bitches, please, fuck that...this is not how it is going down."

As he made his last thought he witnessed something even he wasn't ready for. Dominique pulled something wrapped in plastic from her oversized bag.

"I know that is not what I think it is, oh fuck!"

Dominique stood holding the item in her hand and began to address the room with the same authority she had witnessed her father use for years.

"I took this head off of Kilo because he owed this for being disloyal to the family. I will take any head off of any muthafucka that crosses this family."

As she was talking she placed Kilo's head wrapped in a clear plastic bag on the table in the center of the great room. You could hear a pin drop in the room.

Since that day the twins have held the family down. They still had to prove themselves but time and prosperity have a way of making believers out of the hardest nigga. Dominique built a reputation of being the more sadistic of the two. Monique was known as the silent assassin, you would never see her coming until your death was evident and niggas just didn't fuck with her. But they all wanted to fuck her, they wanted fuck them both.

THIS SHIT IS PERSONAL

Special Agent Beverly believed the problem with street niggas is they think they are invincible; like Superman or some shit. She grew up around these type niggas, her step pops, uncles, even dudes she went to school with, well guess what, all they asses are locked up now. Guess that invincible shit is not what it used to be. She was in the Norfolk field office of the FBI with her feet kicked up on her desk contemplating her next move against GOD's army. The activity that normally plagued the office was nonexistent today because it was Saturday and Agents believed in their weekends. Well almost every agent, but Beverly had some things she wanted to work out in her case, and she couldn't wait until Monday to do it. She found herself lost in thought as she reminisced on her take down of the infamous GOD.

The look on his face when the battering ram hit the door was priceless. Pieces of door went flying in every direction and the agents went running though the opening guns drawn and making their presence felt. GOD never expected anybody to roll up in his crib and take his freedom; well he had never met a bitch like Special Agent Lucinda Beverly. She was the last to step through the opening made by the battering ram. The first thing Beverly noticed was how beautiful the color scheme in the mansion was. Chocolate browns and muted golds were prominent throughout. This was her first time actually in the home but Beverly had cruised through the Estate Mansion section of Virginia Beach on many occasions. She silently marveled at the stunning but traditional mansion.

From her research she knew that the home had a first floor detached master suite, two great rooms, a gourmet kitchen, a study, and several balconies. The 5,300 square foot home had 5 bedrooms and 4 and a half bathrooms.

Beverly remembered wondering why one man needed 5 bedrooms and 4 bathrooms and found herself getting pissed as she usually did when she thought about GOD.

As she continued through the grand entrance of the foyer she felt the excitement building in the pit of her stomach. She wanted to savor this feeling like a smooth brandy as it glides down your throat the first time. Ever since her boss allowed her to set up a special task force and target whoever she felt was the biggest threat on the East Coast Beverly had been dreaming about this day. Special Agent Beverly could have had her choice of targets but she knew from the moment the words left her superior's mouth who she would go after. This shit was personal although she didn't share that with her team.

Walking deeper into the magnificent home Beverly assured herself GOD was a viable target and fit the profile which made all her shit fall under the color of the law. The look on GOD's face would strike fear in a normal bitch, but Special Agent Beverly was far from normal.

As she made it to where the other members of her team were it was obvious they had interrupted GOD relaxing; the surround sound had Frankie Beverly and Maze's "Happy Feeling" playing softly.

*The 70 inch Samsung Plasma mounted over the fireplace
had the football game playing with the volume on mute. A
bottle of Ciroc Ultra- Premium and a half- filled glass
with ice sat on the end table in the sunken great room.
GOD sat with his feet kicked up on his ottoman staring at
his uninvited guests with contempt. Beverly didn't get
the rush of frustration and heat from him she had hoped
for. Even with a house full of agents invading his
personal space he was still let them know he was "that
nigga".*

*What Agent Beverly didn't know was GOD had
witnessed her and the other agents pull onto his street in
their not so undercover government assigned Crown
Vics. He had this whole street wired with surveillance
and would never be caught slipping. He never shit where
he ate so he wasn't worried about anything illegal being
in his home. He made two phone calls. Both were to his
seeds. They knew what to do from there. Of course
Dominique wanted to come over and shoot it out with the
intruders but would back her father's play which was to
get Hawkins on it and chill. Monique assured her father
the money would keep moving and they would get in
contact with Hawkins. The battering ram was
unnecessary, all they had to do was ring and he would
have granted them entrance. GOD was pissed they
destroyed his property but knew it was done to get a rise
out of him so he gave them the exact opposite. He was
chilling on the couch when the agents entered
brandishing their weapons and screaming for no good
damn reason.*

All GOD wanted to know was what the fuck they were doing in his motherfucking house, but all he got from the very attractive agent that had joined the group of idiots coming into the great room and standing in front of GOD was a very tart,

"Shut your fucking mouth! You not the boss of shit right now."

The tone of her voice was something GOD had never had to deal with from anybody, let alone a bitch. GOD looked at Beverly with his Gurkha Black Dragon cigar hanging from his mouth, the look in his eyes didn't give away the danger she was in and before anyone could decipher the message GOD leapt from his seated position and wrapped both of his large football sized hands around her throat attempting to end her life. GOD was squeezing her neck as he lifted her body into the air and swung her from side to side. Agent Beverly couldn't get any air but was attempting to kick out in order to save her own life as she wondered what the fuck her crew was doing.

Agent Patrick and Agent Pennington who had left the great room briefly to check out the other rooms didn't initially know Beverly was in any danger. It wasn't until they heard GOD say "Bitch I will end you!" that they rushed back into the great room. At this point, GOD was only minutes from putting an end to Agent Beverly's life.

Both Agents quickly maneuvered the short distance and put the smack down on him. GOD released Beverly and she fell to the floor and rolled around attempting to regain her strength before she also joined in on the beat down. GOD is far from a punk and he was holding his own. In a way that shit made Beverly kind of proud, but fuck that, she wanted his ass handled at this point; shit he just tried to kill her ass.

The three agents and GOD destroyed the great room as they all showed their skill and refusal to give in. It wasn't until Beverly broke off from the mayhem and retrieved her Glock from its secured place and put it to the back of GOD's head did the activities in the room come to an end. Special Agent Beverly didn't want to kill him, she felt as though she had enough inside shit on GOD to put his ass away for life, and that's just what she planned to do.

During the take down, GOD never showed any fear, in fact he gave as good as he got and still had a look on his face that was almost regal. GOD allowed the agents to sit him down in his enormous kitchen right in front of Beverly. She looked around the gourmet kitchen and marveled at its sight. At the Knotty Alder cabinets, Wolf island steamer, double ovens and Travertine tiles throughout. She even noticed the walk-in wine cellar that held up to 500 bottles. All of this luxury only served to make her more heated. Even though she was pissed, she held the most confident look GOD had seen on any woman other than the two women he loved, his twins. It both puzzled him and excited him at the same time.

He decided to see if he could shake her resolve. He scanned his kitchen and noticed the other agents were close at hand not willing to give him a second chance at killing the beautiful agent. He starred straight into her face and asked as smoothly as he could,

"Fuck you think you got on me little one?"

Beverly was taken off guard a little by his demeanor; she didn't understand how he could be so calm after she just had a Glock to his head. She wanted him to show some kind of emotion.

"Don't you worry yourself with that Mr. Dunbar, but take a look around your lovely home." She gestured her hands around the home and turned to marvel at it again herself before she continued, "Because you will not see it again, it will most likely be seized and sold at auction. I might even buy it myself. I deserve something like this" She actually smiled when that thought sprung from her mouth.

Agent Beverly had a look of extreme satisfaction on her face that told GOD this was personal. She had a look in her eyes he had seen before, the look was of vengeance and it was not a look that should be carried by an agent who was just doing her job. The other two agents in the room didn't have the same look. Sure they looked pissed because they were getting their asses beat, but they still didn't look like GOD had done something to them personally. GOD watched Agent Beverly closely as she continued to stare around his kitchen.

He couldn't put his finger on it, but he knew there was more to this story so he decided to come at the agent from a direction she wouldn't be prepared for. GOD laughed as loud as he could, like the agent had just told a joke.

"Let's go little one, take me downtown so I can get back home before halftime."

Beverly stopped in the middle of her gaze at the granite countertops wondering what the fuck was so damn funny. What did his ass have to laugh about, she was about to bury him under the prison and then destroy his precious daughters as well. GOD was still laughing when the agents led him from his mansion and placed him into the government issued black Crown Victoria with puzzled expressions on their faces.

Beverly remembered that day as if it was yesterday. Still reclined in her office she also recalled the relief she thought would come never fully evolved. Beverly is from the streets so she used the streets to do what the Norfolk PD should have been doing. Her elite team of FBI agents created an inside man who turned on GOD. Sitting up and turning her computer on to access the file Operation DOG; her play on GOD's name, she laughed to herself when she remembered how they turned one of GODS Army against him.

The agents had been tailing their "mark" for 3 months getting a real feel for the shit he was into and boy was it a lot. The FBI had him on their radar for a couple of years because of his reputation as a cleaner. Normally the FBI would work jointly with local law enforcement to bring down a hit man of his caliber, but Agent Beverly knew he was her way into GOD's organization and talked her superiors into allowing her team to make the case against him. She presented it to her boss as too sensitive a case to allow local law enforcement to be a part of due to the level of corruption within their departments.

The reconnaissance mission her team was on was the ground work for the mission. They knew everything the "mark" did from the time he got up each morning until he closed his eyes that night. The agents knew all the women he was fucking from wifey to side chick 1, 2, and 3. Thanks to him they knew where GOD's stash houses were, the playas in the game and where they fell in the chain of command. They even watched a couple of beat downs from a distance.

One beat down was particularly gruesome. The agents followed the "mark" to a townhouse in the Lake Edward section of Virginia Beach. Lake Edwards or LE as it was affectionately known by those who frequent it was off of Lake Edwards Dr. and either Newtown Rd. or Baker Rd depending on what end you were coming in from. During the daytime the area didn't appear to be more than a middle class neighborhood with mostly two story three bedroom townhomes with approximately 1500 square feet of living space in them.

The average home in this area were selling for around $66,000 but majority of the properties were section 8 rentals. The crime in the area was notorious and it was a nightly ritual to hear gun shots and screams. The 'no snitching' code of the street was what the *residents lived by. This allowed crime and decay to run rampant through the neighborhood. The 'mark' had four other guys in the SUV with him. Agent Patrick was snapping pictures and Pennington was rolling video while Beverly drove the vehicle. She wasn't sure who the other fools were in the Escalade or where they would end up, but she knew something was about to go down.*

Beverly followed the driver as he made a left onto Margate Ave right off of Lake Edward Dr. and drove all the way to the back. On Margate Ave the townhouse are located on the left and right. Agent Beverly didn't want to blow up the spot, so once she turned onto Margate she made a quick right into a large parking lot that was utilized by 8 townhouses. She backed her vehicle into a parking spot and from where they sat they could see everything.

It was midnight and the streets were alive, but for some reason Margate Ave was quiet. The 'mark' jumped out of the cocaine white Escalade looking like new money. Agent Beverly couldn't hide the smile on her face when she noticed he was wearing one of the twins men's white velour Make Money sweat suits with a pair of white on white Bulldogs from their Double Take clothing line. Double Take was one of the legitimate businesses the twins had that Beverly was attempting to find a way to destroy. Putting her hate aside Beverly had to admit the man wearing the clothes was filling them out damn good.

She didn't even realize she was speaking out loud until it was too late. She had binoculars up to her face aimed at the 'mark' as he stood in front of the Escalade "Damn he is doing it, I can't even front he fine as shit and if he wasn't a fuck up he could get it." Agent Patrick starred at the side of Beverly's face and the look on Patrick's face showed his disapproval, but he tried to hide it just as soon as it appeared. He turned away from her and looked into the face of his other partner. The look on Patrick's face did not go unnoticed by Agent Pennington, who disagreed as well but for different reasons. Pennington just hunched his shoulders and shook his head and turned his attention back to the men gathering around the SUV.

The "mark" looked around surveying his area; the street was pretty much clear. He was unaware that he was being watched by federal agents. He gathered his crew and they made their way to the brown door with the welcome mat on the ground and without knocking kicked the door off the hinges.

The agents all sat back looking at each other with surprise and anticipation, "Damnnnn!" they said in unison. They all retuned their focus to the door that was leaning to the side halfway still together "Did you see that shit?" Patrick asked, adding "These niggas think they are Rambo!"

Special Agent Beverly wasn't surprised because she knew some funky shit was about to jump off. She leaned closer with her binoculars saying over her shoulder, "Just don't stop the video. This shit is about to get funky."

Fanita Moon Pendleton

The sounds in the home were unrecognizable to the agent's vantage point in the utility work truck that they used for surveillance purposes. Before they had to think of another plan the 'mark' and his crew came out of the door dragging a dude who looked like his name should be Fat Albert. He was huge all around from his large head to protruding belly. Beverly could see why at least three of them were dragging his ass, he was enormous. The man being dragged hit his head on the concrete and he yelled out in pain. Everything was happening in slow motion and the agents got it all on video and still camera.

The pace picked up when a naked woman ran through battered front door with her breasts sagging and carrying a large extra pouch. She ran up to the men holding her man captive attempting to plead for his life. She was stopped by the silenced shot from one of the goons .38. The bullet left a hole right in the middle of her forehead. The "mark" looked around the neighborhood to make sure it was all good just as her body hit the pavement.

The agents were ready to jump out on these fools and wrap this shit up, but Beverly saw the bigger picture. She held her hand in the air as Pennington was reaching for the door.

"Look we are not stopping shit. We are here for the bigger picture and all this shit would be happening whether we were here or not. If his ass is out here doing this shit you can believe GOD sanctioned it and I WANT GOD!"

She said the shit with so much conviction both agents sat back and stared at her unsure of where all of the emotion was coming from. They had known Beverly for years, been part of the same Seal Team, did many operations together for the Bureau, but they had never seen her so personally invested in a case. They shared a look between themselves, shrugged their shoulders and turned their attention back to their assignment deciding to follow Beverly's lead.

Special Agent Beverly felt they had GOD's ass now. She appreciated her team for backing her play. She knew they had questions but they were questions she could not answer. All they had to do was hem the 'mark' up and he would lead them to the promised land. Everybody appeared to be on the same page, although Agents Patrick and Pennington, or the DP's, as Beverly affectionately called them. felt a certain way about just letting shit happen they knew what their main goal was. A loud scream brought everyone's attention back to the beat down that was occurring in front of them.

Fat Albert screamed so loud when he saw his woman hit the ground with that dot in her head that there was no way someone didn't hear it, but this was Lake Edwards. Screams in the middle of the night, gunshots, fights, and death are nothing new to this neighborhood and in LE the code of the street is honored. Mind your own damn business, and no snitching. So although the piercing scream was surely heard, you can be assured no one called the cops.

The 'mark' punched Fat Albert in his neck and dared him to scream again as he was dragged to the Escalade, but from somewhere deep in his soul Fat Albert decided he was going to make a stand right there and began to fight. He was large and although the 'mark' was not a small man in stature he was no match for a man like Fat Albert once he realized he had nothing else to live for.

Fat Albert threw 'the mark' off of him so easily and swiftly you would have thought he was 100 pounds lighter. Before he could make another move the same goon that put a hole in his woman's head, put the barrel of the Glock to his head. Fat Albert knew his time was up and he had no more fight in him. He dropped to his knees and waited for blackness to invade his body and end his life. Instead he was grabbed by the crew and harshly marched to the Escalade and violently pushed into the back of the truck. The 'mark' got off of the ground and with a deep scowl on his face brushed off his clothes and without another word the crew jumped in the truck and headed out. The agents looked at each other in astonishment, but Beverly put the vehicle in gear and she followed them out of the neighborhood.

The Escalade traveled down Newtown Rd and hopped on Interstate 264E with the agents a couple of car lengths behind them. Everyone in the undercover vehicle was deep in thought; no one wanted to admit that something was fucked up.

Special Agent Beverly was grabbing the steering wheel so hard her knuckles began to turn white. She wasn't questioning her actions, she was wondering where the fuck they were going as they merged onto 64E but when the Escalade took exit 14A towards Interstate 664N Agent Beverly knew they were heading out of town.

Pennington who was the most politically correct out of the trio asked, "Do you think we should call for back up?" He looked from Beverly to Patrick in an attempt to gauge their feelings before he said, "At least call in the murder in Lake Edwards?" Everyone appeared to be giving his ideas some thought. Patrick who was now sitting in the passenger seat of the utility van was quiet and staring out the window contemplating and thinking that Pennington had a good point. Beverly however; didn't want the locals messing up her knock either by just plain fucking up or by leaking information. She looked to her right at Patrick and then in her rearview mirror at Pennington and said, "I'm going to pull rank on this one, for the integrity of the case we will leave the locals out of this part of it. I am sure they are on the murder scene by now; they don't need to know of our interest in the case."

Both agents knew Beverly would be thinking of the case first so they didn't readily disagree with her once she put it like that. They didn't normally disagree with her because she never steered them wrong. Before they could discuss it further they were taking Exit 291B towards Elizabeth City, NC. The smile on Beverly's face was so electric Patrick had to take notice.

"Hell you smiling like that for Bev?"

*Beverly hit the dashboard and whistled loudly saying,
"Because, they are heading to the state of North
Carolina and straight into our jurisdiction."*

*Once the Escalade crosses over the Virginia line
and enters North Carolina any crimes they commit, even
the crime of transporting the victim, all fall under federal
jurisdiction. The atmosphere in the vehicle was alive and
the agents were ready to make their move. All they
needed was for the Escalade to merge onto US 17 South
crossing into North Carolina.*

*"BINGO!" Special Agent Beverly yelled as both
vehicles passed the Welcome to North Carolina sign.
Beverly smiled to herself because she remembered the
North Carolina website says North Carolina "A Better
Place" she told her partners this saying, "I think it's
ironic the criminals are bringing Fat Albert to "A Better
Place" to make his departure from this life." Pennington
laughed but all of them agreed they would stop the crime
from continuing before another death occurred. With the
video tape and still camera shots they had enough on
everyone in the vehicle to put them away in a federal
prison for the rest of their lives.*

*As the Escalade turned into a heavily rural area
and parked the FBI team prepared for their take down.
Agent Patrick secured the weapons and Special Agent
Beverly pulled the vehicle over to keep out of sight, she
would let the night offer shelter. Beverly turned to her
team "Ok let's go on foot from here, I want to take them
by surprise and catch them before they hurt his ass."*

She continued to prepare to make the bust that would get her one step closer to her goal of taking down GOD himself. Both agents Patrick and Pennington were in the zone, and they were in synch like they always were. Bullet proof vests were snapped, Glocks were secured, and swagger was on point. The team made their way into the shadows using a full tactical approach.

The high beams of the Escalade were illuminating the entire rural back drop and Fat Albert could be heard begging for his life. The team wanted to flank the group who were all focused on humiliating their victim, but Beverly held her hand up giving direction using their Navy Seal hand signals. She wanted to listen for a minute to glean as much unsolicited information as she could.

The 'mark' could be heard yelling at the top of his lungs, "Where the fuck is the dope and money Geno?" It was a question being asked but no time was given for Geno which was Fat Albert's real name to answer the question before he could be heard screaming like a banshee. He was pinned to a large oak tree with a knife sticking through both legs and one in each shoulder; this was a sick game of torture that 'mark' had mastered over the years. The other goons looked on in appreciation and amazement. They had heard rumors about what they were witnessing but never had the privilege to see it up close and personal. Each had a look of appreciation on their faces as 'mark' raised another knife ready to cause more damage.

Geno was losing consciousness, the sweat pouring from his face was mixed with blood and dripping fast. The amount of blood loss would have finished a less nourished man at a more rapid pace, but Geno was attempting to hold his own. The agents were well within the kill zone and had formulated a plan of attack. Patrick smiled and imagined himself back in combat with his Seal family, a feeling that always gave him strength.

The approach was flawless; their Seal training was evident with the lack of detection by the goons, but the "mark" felt their approach in his gut. He was not Seal trained but he was street tested and he made a run for the woods before the agents could fully pull their Glocks.

"Fuck!" Beverly let out as she took off into the woods behind him, leaving her team to deal with the other men and getting Geno some help. The woods were nothing new to her, she felt most at home in the darkness and dampness that lie ahead. She would have preferred the approach to have not been detected and silently thought about putting her team through some much needed refresher training. Beverly knew he would make a run for the highway and attempt to hitch a ride so she made her way in the direction of the highway.

The lights of the highway were straight ahead and the sounds of passing motorists assured Beverly she was in the right area. She emerged from the thick brush just in time to see several tractor trailers pull out onto the highway.

"Fuck, I know his ass is in one of them fucking rigs. But that's alright, I'm going to get his ass because I know where to find him." These things were running though her mind as she continued to glare up and down the road squinting to see if the 'mark' would slip up even though she knew he wouldn't.

Beverly radioed her crew, who were wrapping up the crime scene with the local law enforcement, who were now aware that the Feds would maintain jurisdiction over this mess and they were both relieved and happy.

"Fellas, I lost him, but we can get him after we get situated because we know exactly where to find him. I am on my way back; let's wrap this up so we can get the fuck out of North Carolina." Beverly turned to head back into the woods and meet back up with her boys. Inside she felt good about where they were in Operation DOG. Within the next month her team should be able to make a solid arrest and she would be able to exact her revenge on GOD.

The team wrapped up in North Carolina and smoothed local law enforcement over. They were pissed because they had to process and hold the three clowns that crossed state lines with the 'mark'. The agents assured them they would be transported to Virginia within the week. Fat Albert was transported to a local hospital and was barely hanging onto life. Agent Pennington made arrangements with the officers to alert them when his condition was stable enough to place him in witness protection. On the way back to Virginia they began to process where they were with the case.

Agent Patrick said to his team "Let's go find this stupid fuck now!" Pennington who had taken over the driving duties took one hand off of the steering wheel and raised it in the air saying "I second that, who the fuck needs sleep, let's get this bastard off of the street tonight!" Both men looked at Beverly to gauge her reaction and just like they expected she was game. She was already in the back of the van getting the weapons ready. They rode the rest of the way back to Virginia in silence.

It took the agents a week to catch up with the 'mark'. He wisely laid low not showing up at any of his regular spots, not even his home. But even the best slip up, they get cabin fever and just have to get out.

Patrick was the first to spot him as he walked across the parking lot headed towards a local hangout called Barry's. "There his ass go right there," Patrick said, causing the other agents to look in the direction he was pointing. The agents knew he would eventually show up here because this is where the hood comes to floss. The watched the 'mark' as he made his way to the door, passed through security, and disappeared through the door. By the show in the parking lot, the entire hood was here tonight. All of the latest big body SUV's and souped-up sports cars were crowded in the lot. This gave the perfect cover for the white utility van parked in the far right corner. Pennington suggested a plan, "Beverly you do your cute girl thang," he winked and Beverly made a fist at him. Laughing he said, "I can't help it if these fools find you irresistible," still laughing he looked towards Patrick to have his back but was confronted with a blank stare.

Beverly agreed with Pennington's assessment because from previous recon, they knew he had two weakness. P and P; the pool table and pussy and as fate would have it Special Agent Beverly held the best hand when it came to both. They all got out of the van and made their way towards the spot. Patrick took care of security dropping him $300 to look the other way, no sweat.

Both Agents Patrick and Pennington were hanging out in their best hood gear looking inconspicuous. Patrick went to the bar and ordered a Hennessey and Coke and Pennington got them a booth and began mingling with the chicks. Beverly went straight to the pool tables and called next. The inside of Barry's was plush, it was a two story spot surrounded by mirrors which made it appear much bigger than it was. There was a large dance floor surrounded by steel cages. Each cage had a near naked woman dancing in it. The cages left enough room between each so those who wanted to access the dance floor could still do so. The dance floor was packed with people sweating and grinding. Chris Brown's latest was blaring from the speakers and everybody was going in. There were two bars downstairs and a large amount of tables and booths. In the far left corner was where the real party was, it was the section dedicated to the pool hustlers. The area was larger than any one Beverly had ever seen in a club. It held four tables but they were nicely spaced and left plenty of room for people to sit around and talk shit.

It was Beverly's time to shoot and the loser of the previous game was racking the table so she could start putting the smack down on niggas at the pool table. She was wearing some shit that would have niggas paying more attention to how heavy their balls were feeling then to the balls she was dropping on the table. When the 'mark' walked into the pool section Beverly had to remind herself what her objective was because the chocolate bar in front of her was looking good enough to eat, and she loved herself some damn chocolate. He was rocking all black Sean Jean with a chest that was standing up like that African nigga in that movie saying "Give us our Free." That chest was just begging to jump out and be fucking free. Beverly felt the tingling sensation in her treasure box that let her know this nigga was dangerous. But she was sure after he realized she had his ass on murder, assault, kidnapping and transportation across state lines in commission of a felony he would see she was the dangerous one. Beverly continued to watch the 'mark' on the sly as her opponent cracked the table, dropping nothing off on the break. Once it was her shot she made quick work of her opponent running seven balls easily. After that first game she continued to run niggas off the table left and right, for a minute she thought he wasn't going to even play. He was taking shots with his crew as they continued to watch her put in work. Beverly watched him walk closer to the table and put his quarter on the table and sit back in the cut talking to his boys. They weren't fooling nobody though because they were all in the crack of her ass. Beverly made sure on the next shot, they got an eyeful as she yelled out

"Eight ball bank to the left corner."

The dude she was playing; some off-brand ass nigga, yelled out bullshit!" The 'mark' stepped out of the corner and said "I put five hundred on shorty making the shot." The off-brand nigga decided he needed to save face and pulled out his gwap and said "This bitch is not making shit!" Beverly felt she had to show this old ass Puma wearing nigga what a real bitch could do. It got quiet as shit near their table and niggas started really paying attention to what was going down. Beverly saw her team out of the corner of her eye along with niggas making side bets like a mutha. She sized up her shot, one she has made a million times. When she bent over the table she heard a nigga make a comment, "Damn that bitch is caked up!" Niggas was laughing and co-signing like a muthafucka.

Beverly decided it was time to put off-brand out of his misery. When the cue ball cracked the eight you could hear a pin drop until the eight-ball rolled into the designated pocket and niggas went wild. The 'mark' walked over to off-brand and snatched his scratch from him talking mad shit, "She bust your ass nigga, give me my shit!" The "mark" tried to give Beverly half.

"Here you go baby girl, your cue game is sick and you earned this."

Beverly shook her head back and forth turning down the money, she walked into his personal space inhaling his tasty scent and in her most seductive voice said "I want you."

She walked away from him and went to grab her pool stick as he realized she was offering him a chance at the crown. He made his move to get his stick and turned towards the off-brand nigga and said, "Bring your dusty ass over here and rack. You know losers rack, and she bust your ass!"

The room erupted in laughter and even Beverly had to laugh at that shit. The 'mark' then turned to her and said "I don't know what you laughing at scrumptious, I am about to bust your ass... don't worry though baby you gonna like how daddy put it down." Niggas started laughing again. He tried to sweeten her up by offering her a drink as they waited for the balls to get racked. Beverly was looking seductive as hell as she sweetly told him "Naw baby I need to be sober for what I'm about to put on you Big Daddy". The co-signers were slapping shoulders and just keeping up a ruckus. He told his boys to bring him some Henn Dog. The crowd in their area grew larger like they knew this was about to be an American Pool League Special.

The DJ must have felt the excitement in the pool area because he hyped the room up by playing DJ Khaled "All I Do is Win." Beverly even got in the grove and started singing that shit as a warning to her opponent.

"All I do is win win win no matter WHAT."

The look on the 'mark's' face was priceless. He watched her hips move from side to side as she moved to the beat and she could tell he was feeling her because she had seen the look many times before.

Most men couldn't concentrate when she was in the place, they were too busy looking at her tight waist, bubble ass and thick thighs. She always used this distraction to her benefit. Her plan was to make this quick and painless, so she broke the balls using all elbow and dropped the eight ball off the break. That shit was magnificent and her mark was in a trance as his eyes followed the eight ball to the side pocket. Niggas went wild and the 'mark' was looking at her like he wanted to fuck. He got in her body space and whispered "Damn ma, you got my dick hard as hell with that shit... you should really let me take this party somewhere private." Beverly faked interest because her objective was to get him alone so she could get him on the team. So she licked her lips and said, "Let's make that happen right now baby." It wasn't hard for him to believe she would be down with it, he considered himself a prime catch, but he still wanted to leave quickly before she changed her mind.

Once they left Barry's he dismissed his crew and told them he would catch up with them in the morning. Beverly and the "mark" decided to get something to eat which was perfect for what she had planned. She noticed that her team was on point so they bounced to Landstown Commons the shopping center with the IHOP in it. This is the best IHOP to come to because it's never crowded. Once they were seated Beverly noticed he kept looking at her funny and she silently hoped he didn't recognize her but decided it didn't matter with what she was about to drop on him. They both picked up their menu's and started looking at the items.

Beverly didn't think they would actually be eating so she was just looking to look. He put his menu down and looked at Beverly and said "You look like I know you from somewhere, but I know we have never met because I would never forget you, I'm sure of that." He scratched his head as if in deep thought.

Shaking her head she slowly placed her menu back on the table as well and said "I am sure you don't know me, but we are about to get to know each other very well." The look on his face was one of pure lust and he couldn't help but let the little head think and assumed Beverly was talking about fucking. She quickly burst his bubble as she recounted the events of a week ago and who she was. The features that were so masculine and handsome before became almost deranged looking but he remained cool because he mistakenly thought she wanted money. His voice was just above a whisper.

"How much you trying to squeeze me for you trifling bitch? You playing a very dangerous game and I'm a very dangerous man." He was now leaning halfway across the table as he made his point.

It was at this point the waitress made her appearance and asked if they were ready to order. Beverly glanced up at the pretty girl, she couldn't have been more than 19 or 20, but surely she had no idea what she had just walked up on. Beverly told her to give them about twenty minutes and then they would be ready to order. The waitress thought that sounded strange and even more the man sitting at the table looked strange.

But she didn't want to get involved so she just said no problem and walked off to tend to her other business. Beverly took this opportunity to address the 'mark.'

"First of all its Special Agent Lucinda Beverly to you and I don't want your fucking money, I want GOD." The rest is history, the agents worked the 'mark' to get all the information and evidence needed to bring down GOD.

Closing the Operation DOG folder on her computer after reviewing everything helped Beverly decide she needed to think deep on how to make a move on the rest of GOD's army. She had been in the office now for five hours and would probably put in another couple of hours before going home. Beverly couldn't help but feel she cut off the head of the snake, but the damn body didn't die. She decided to get back on her game. The personal shit had her slipping. Standing up to stretch her tired legs, she thought about the twins. She hated the twins but she really couldn't put into words why she hated them so much because they hadn't done anything to her personally. She moved towards the window and stared out into the beautiful sun driven day and began to reminisce on where the hatred all began.

Growing up shit could have gone one way or another for Beverly and her mother Laverne. Her pops didn't want to have anything to do with them and in the beginning they were scrambling just to make it. Laverne was a real determined type of chick and she tried to reason with the father of her child to at least take care of them, at least be there for Beverly.

She even told him she didn't want anything from him romantically she just didn't want to be out scrambling with a baby. But Laverne told Beverly he basically said fuck her and fuck the kid too. They scrambled for a while until her mom met Larry. He stepped in and became the man of the house. Where they were going to live and what they were going to eat was no longer the problem. Laverne and Larry had a son. Beverly was happy to have a little brother, someone to call her own who would depend on and look up to her.

Larry was hood and he never met a con he thought he couldn't pull, but he loved Beverly and always encouraged her to do shit differently than the average chick. Beverly had to give him props for that. Shit was a struggle still because Larry stayed getting locked up but she will always give him the credit for being there. Laverne was sure to give Beverly yearly updates on her real dad but Beverly didn't really care much about him until her mother revealed he had twin girls. Laverne was bitter about being dumped by GOD and she made sure her daughter shared that hate, and with the knowledge that he had two daughters who he decided were worth keeping the foundation was solid. Beverly knew it would be hard work to be successful but she was determined to do it just so she could show her no show daddy she was worth it.

Beverly felt very sad after remembering her childhood and decided it was time to leave the office and try and enjoy a weekend for once so she gathered her stuff and went home.

MONIQUE

Dominique ran GOD's army with Jamal; they were responsible for all security issues and disciplinary needs. Dominique knew Jamal had a thing for her, but although he was fine as shit, Dominique wasn't convinced he was what she needed, she felt she needed a man more like her father. Monique dealt directly with the connect in North Carolina and made sure everybody ate and the connect was always happy.

Monique also ensured she and Dominique were diversified in legitimate businesses. The twin's organization Double Take Incorporated had several holdings to include Make Money clothing, Bulldog shoes, single family homes, apartment complexes, and shopping centers. These properties were owned outright and the company employed several people to manage the holdings on a daily basis. The main office for Double Take Incorporated was located in a new luxury building just built in the Ghent section of Norfolk.

Monique was sitting in the study in her home in the Sand Bridge Beach section of Virginia Beach. Sand Bridge is a coastal community located on the northern end of the Outer Banks. Monique loved the seclusion and the privacy the area offers. There is only one public access road that leads into the community. Her 9 bedroom 10 bathroom retreat on the beach is far removed from the hustle and bustle of the street. This was her sanctuary and no one knew where she lived but her most trusted soldiers. Monique never conducted business in her home; she kept all of the grime in the streets.

The walls in the study were covered from floor to ceiling with every kind of book imaginable and Monique had read them all. She was the more studious of the two but just as deadly as Dominique. The solid mahogany desk that Monique sat behind was her father's. The Monte Carlo L Desk was something to marvel at with its marble columns, ash panels, and detailed carvings. She was always fascinated by how fabulously detailed and lavishly decorated the desk was.

Monique sipped on Ciroc Red Berry as she remembered sitting around this very desk and watching her father conduct business and school his daughters in the art of strategy.

"Baby girl, you got to always be one step, fuck that, two steps ahead of your enemies and competition. It is their job to catch you slipping and your job to ensure that they don't. Look at every situation from every possible angle and always anticipate what your competition will do."

Monique had looked into her father's eyes as he spoke to her somehow knowing what he was telling her would one day save her life. She couldn't have been more than 13 years old but she knew this was serious.

"Anticipate what your own people are doing and thinking as well. Many a powerful man has been brought to his knees by his woman or his best friend."

Monique knew someone was on the verge of challenging GOD's territory. Word on the street is that the twins were weak.

Monique could not understand why anyone would assume they would fold under pressure. They had no idea how deadly GOD's army or the twins were. Monique and Dominique were not just deadly because they were so skillful but because they were thinkers, planners and organizers of ideas. *"We are respected by their crew and feared by their counterparts, all except whoever this dumb fool is,"* Monique thought.

There are some who still believe the twin's true power comes from the sweat and tears of their father. Some believe the respect and the fear people have for the twins comes strictly from the respect and fear everyone has for GOD. That will be the downfall of the so called take over. It is true everyone fears GOD, but the twins can hold their own because GOD taught them everything they need to know in order to do it and do it right.

It had been two months since GOD was arrested. Monique by design laid low to ensure the money kept flowing without a hitch. Today the twins are meeting with the top lieutenants to discuss the strategy that will be used to find out who the threat is; and how to end it. Monique sat behind her father's desk and thought about the different ways to approach the situation. Shadow would be their biggest lead. His dumb ass got spotted following Dominique and he would eventually lead them straight to whoever he was working for. He was a killer with a murder game to match their own and would have to be watched closely.

He didn't even know his tail had been compromised so he was definitely not as smart as the twins. Monique kicked around several ideas of how they might come at them thinking,

"I guess people assume since GOD is on lockdown that the whole cut off the head of the snake and the rest will follow is what's up, but they don't know that this family has planned for this for years. They won't catch us slipping though; I am going to beef up the professional and private security for the family heads."

Monique figured the next thing to do is to hit everyone else in their pocket. "See niggas don't understand shit until you fuck with their money," she thought to herself. The idea was to show VA that ain't shit stopped because GOD was on lockdown. GOD's army supplies over 90% of the crews in the area. Monique was about to create a drought, except in her crew. The drought will continue until muthafuckas flushed out the bad seed.

"If muthafuckas want to eat, somebody better say something."

Monique thought about what other advantages a drought would have,

"This will allow me to see who is making money without using my product, if someone other than my family is still making moves then that is the one I need to be seeing."

Monique put the finishing touches on the plan and stood up and smoothed out her Dolce pencil skirt before grabbing her leg to make sure her tiny .22 pistol was there. She also looked inside of her Marc Jacob bag to ensure her Glock was there and ready to roll. She grabbed her Marc Jacob glasses and slipped on her Manolo stilettos and was ready to head out the door. Monique looked back at a picture on her desk of her and her father in the midst of a heated session and could only smile, *"I'm doing what you taught me to do Daddy."*

In the sunken great room there were four guys that all looked like they should be playing in the NFL. Collectively they were known as the Hit Squad. They were all ex-Navy Seals by trade, but they all grew up in the tidewater area of the seven cities. Marcus, Monique's head of security was the son of God's best friend Michael. Monique and Marcus grew up as close as siblings. Monique wanted to sit on Marcus's face so bad she creamed every time she saw him. He had the look of Ray Lewis with the swagger of Idris Elba, quiet and mysterious. His low cut Cesar gave him a sophisticated look and the silhouette in his pants assured her he was working with a monster.

Marcus and Monique had been intimate many times but never had sex. Monique dreamed about the day Marcus would take her virginity and fill her up with the thickness that was promised by the bulge in his slacks. Monique was feeling a little warm.

"Weeee ok let me get back to the task at hand."

She continued deeper into the great room to approach Marcus. Monique didn't normally speak to the other members of the Hit Squad because Marcus had it set up all communication went through him.

"I wonder why that is?" she thought. She actually preferred it that way anyway so no need to bitch.

"Marcus. I need to get to a meeting in Norfolk."

Marcus was looking so deep into her eyes she wasn't sure if he had heard her or not but just when she was about to say something he said,

"I got you Mo."

Marcus is the only one that called her Mo. Marcus had been calling her Mo since they were 5 years old. It would shock Monique if he ever called her anything else. She gave him the smile that was only reserved for him and he winked and turned to his crew and began giving orders. His tone was firm but not argumentative and everyone began to hop to it. Within seconds they were ready to roll in the bullet proof Lexus SUVs that were parked in the circular driveway. Today Monique wanted to ride in the middle vehicle. She never rode in the same position and Marcus never made the decision which vehicle she would ride in until they walked out of the door.

When Monique stepped outside she could feel the sun kiss her butter pecan skin and send a tingle down her neck.

"Damn that feels good."

Monique looked towards the vehicles and could see they had just finished up the inspection of the inside, outside, and underneath.

Marcus said, "Mo let's take the lead truck to Norfolk."

Although she wanted to ride in the middle, she didn't argue with Marcus. First of all he wasn't having that shit, but secondly she trusted his judgment so she proceeded to the lead vehicle.

While they rested in the back of the truck Marcus began to reflect on his life since retirement from the Navy. Marcus was the best at what he did. He was a strategic thinker and kept his emotions at bay in order to accomplish a mission. His time in the Navy put him in situations that would make the average man drop down into a fetal position and start sucking his thumb. The skills Marcus and his team possessed were really lacking a market in the real world. When GOD first approached him to head security for his organization and be the personal body guard of one of his daughters Marcus immediately chose Mo. Keeping her safe was more than just a promise he had made to GOD and his own father. Marcus had his own agenda for keeping Mo safe. She was everything to him and he loved everything about her, always had and always would. Monique represented so many first for Marcus. No other woman understood him so completely and dealt with him with no judgment. The things Mo and Marcus shared still made him long for her on many a lonely night. His thoughts were not just sexual, they represented forever.

"Mo understands me and that's just that. I don't know if I can protect her fully if I reveal what's going on in my heart." Marcus was brought back to earth by Mo saying something he couldn't make out.

"Marcus you are not even listening to me. Your body is here with me, but I'm not sure about your mind." She sucked her teeth and folded her arms across her ample chest. Marcus couldn't help but laugh at the look of agitation across Mo's face "I'm right here Mo. What you say?"

She blew out a frustrated breath and asked "Who is she Marcus?"

Marcus shot his eyebrow to the sky and gave Mo a sly grin, "Why you want to know Mo? What are you going to do to her?"

The arms fell from her chest and she sat up straight in her seat "Oh you think this is funny Marcus. ok. Don't get the bitch fucked up, you know I am not playing."

The laughter that erupted from Marcus took Monique by surprise; she couldn't remember the last time she heard him laugh. The deep baritone of it sent a tingle right to her most sensitive spot before she knew it she had said "Damn." out loud with a look of sensuality on her face.

Marcus pushed the button on the window that divided the driver and the back seat so he could have privacy.

With one quick motion he circled Monique's lips with his tongue and her panties became instantly soaked. He looked into Mo's eyes and asked her again "Why you want to know Mo?"

Trying desperately to stop inhaling the perfect scent of man it took everything in her to say "Stop playing with me Marcus. You know I don't like that."

Now holding her close in his arms he calmly asked, "What do you like Mo? Tell me baby. What do you like?"

Looking her best friend in his beautiful eyes, "We don't have enough time for what I like." The seductive sound of her voice held a question and a challenge.

"Oh really?" Marcus winked at her, their silent signal and with that he laid her gently on the black leather and he got on his knees. When he pulled down her panties and realized they were soaked through he began to smell them and grinned from ear to ear.

"Damn momma is this all for me?"

Monique's eyes were so glassy you would have thought she was crying but that's just the passion this man had brought out in her since she was 13 years old. Marcus took her legs and hooked them over his shoulders and began to circle her clit with intensity yet so gently that she instantly nutted. He licked every fold and all the sweet juices gushed from her insides.

"Mo, I love how hard your clit gets when I put it in my mouth."

Monique wanted to say something but she was frozen in a state of passion that could only be brought out by one man. Marcus licked all of her juices like it was his last meal. He loved the taste of Monique, every time he tasted her he dreamed about it for days after.

"Damn Mo, you taste so good "

Monique finally regained her composure enough to participate in the conversation.

"I ... I love it Marcus."

Marcus kissed up Monique's thighs until he got to her lips, he sucked her lips deep and sensually. He trailed kisses up to her ear; until he could hear the deep sensual moans coming from her throat. He sucked her ear and revealed to her something he had been holding in his heart for too long.

"I love you Mo."

Their eyes met and locked in position, neither one saying anything, but for different reasons. Monique was lost in thought about what it would mean to give her heart and her soul to someone else. Marcus's mind wondered if pursuing the love he knew was in his heart would put Monique's life in jeopardy. Neither one of them was ready to throw caution to the wind and be what each other needed most. He sat up and put Mo's panties in his pocket just as they were pulling up to their destination. He sat Monique back up and took his seat back next to her. With a wink he said.

"Told you we would have enough time."

Monique couldn't do anything but laugh because she knew if she could ever experience anything like love it was Marcus she would experience it with.

"I heard what you said Marcus."

Marcus's eyes tightened but held a light that was reserved only for her.

"I know you did, now what are we going to do about it?"

Monique started to answer but one of the crew opened the back door for her to step out and she watched Marcus get out of the car and go around to the other side. Monique thought to herself, *"Oh we gonna talk about this again real soon cause I needs to feel that dick. And I know his ass won't give it to me until we have had that talk."* Although Marcus had tasted Monique on several occasions he would not make love to her. *"Hell right about now I would settle for a fuck was all Monique could think."* But she knew Marcus and she knew he loved her. He had told her on more than one occasion that when she was ready to take that next step with him she would have to let him know.

"Damnnnn, am I ready? Can I trust him? Will he always hold me down?" These are questions deep down inside she already knew the answers to, but watching her dad hurt over the years from the loss of her mother, she didn't want to experience that same type of heartache herself.

This had stopped her from giving herself emotionally to any man, hell she hasn't really given herself physically either. Hearing Dominique's laughter brought Monique back to the present.

GOD'S ARMY

They were at the Norfolk Airport Hilton in a penthouse suite. The suite was huge and had a conference room, a full dining room, a living room, a fully stocked kitchen, a theater room, and 3 bedrooms with attached bathrooms. A seafood buffet was set up in the dining room with everything from lobster, crab legs, and fried and steamed shrimp. When Monique walked in most of GOD's army were already there. GOD's army consisted of the main lieutenants. The foot soldiers did not have the distinction of being in GOD's army but they all had aspirations.

There were 10 lieutenants and each of them had 20 soldiers underneath them. It was each lieutenant's responsibility to be in control of their crew and develop their own chain of command. Each lieutenant get their orders from Jamal who is over all the lieutenants and Jamal gets his orders from the twins. This meeting today was not a normal thing. The main point of the meeting was to allow the lieutenants to voice their concerns in the territory they monitor and have those concerns addressed. After the larger meeting the lieutenants will retire to have dinner while Monique, Dominique, Marcus and Jamal had their strategic meeting.

Monique noticed her Uncle Dollar in the room and didn't know why he was there. He was no longer functioning as a lieutenant. His demotion was gradual and had more to do with his relationship with GOD than anything else.

Dollar is GOD's baby brother. He reminded Monique of her father in so many ways physically, but mentally Uncle Dollar couldn't hold a candle to her pops. Where GOD was smart, strategic, and methodical Dollar tripped over his words and couldn't tie his own shoes if his big brother wasn't there to help him. Dollar was a ladies' man and had all the girls wrapped around his 6'4 frame.

Dollar noticed the way his niece was looking at him. He knew the relationship with his nieces was not good. They didn't respect him and he knew it. It wasn't always like that though, he could remember when the twins loved him and he would do anything for him.

Birthdays were always a special time for the Dunbar clan and the twins loved when their Uncle Dollar came into the house with damn near the whole Toys R Us following him. When the girls heard him come through the door they ran down the stairs so fast that Dominique jumped the final three steps almost giving Monique a heart attack, but making Dollar laugh.

"Dom you are going to be the gangsta out of the two of you that's for sure."

The smile Dollar had in his eyes was the pride he felt for his nieces and the love he secretly held for their mother Jewel. "Damn I miss seeing her," he thought, "but seeing the girls is just like looking at her." Just as those thoughts crossed his mind GOD walked into the room with a look of disgust written on his face that he would not verbalize.

"Dollar, why you buy all this shit? You know my seeds got more than they need."

Dollar hid his true feelings behind his smile as he picked up Dominique and gave her a big hug.

"Come on Lawrence you know I got to hook my nieces up, these are my girls and they need to know Uncle Dollar got them."

The girls were too engrossed in thinking about opening up all of their new gifts and were really too young to understand the tension in the room so they jumped up and down and hugged their uncle's neck.

Dollar knew GOD had a problem with the way the girls responded to him but he didn't give a fuck. He knew as long as his nieces had his back GOD would always keep him around. Dollar played on the girl's love for him and he made sure he was always there for them.

Dollar didn't know GOD only kept him around because of the deep respect he had for Pops Dunbar. Dollar didn't believe GOD knew about any of his shady behavior and thought his brother was still upset over Jewel's death.

Dollar was shocked out of his daydream by the sound of music and laughter. He had a look on his face that said, *"Don't fuck with me."* He thought about what he needed to do and how it needed to go down. Dollar thought about his relationship with his nieces as he watched them from a dark corner in the massive room.

Monique, damn if she is not Jewel all over again. The way she carries herself with the self-confidence of a man, but the femininity of royalty, damn I miss Jewel. And look at that damn Dominique weewwww... yeah she is her momma's daughter, but at the same time it's like looking Lawrence straight in the face.

Dollar thought the girls were spoiled asses who thought it was all about them. He planned on showing them that the torch is supposed to be passed to the next male in the family not no bitches. He rubbed his week old stubble and attempted to be rational *"I know they are my nieces but they need to fall back and let me run this."*

Dollar planned on meeting with the girls tonight when he could get them alone to make his demands. He was shut out of the Lieutenants meeting and that was pissing him off even more "Who the fuck do they think they are? I helped their fucking daddy built this shit!" He roared around the room while the meeting was taking place down the hall.

The biggest issue brought out in the meeting with the lieutenants was their desire to recruit more soldiers to swell their ranks past the 20 soldier limit. Monique who studied business while at Hampton University and had been running not only their legitimate businesses but the business side of GOD's army for a number of years explained to the group the basis behind span of control. The term originating in military organization theory; it refers to the number of subordinates a supervisor can effectively supervise. Too many soldiers would create a management nightmare and reduce the lieutenant's ability to run a tight ship.

It was like a light bulb went off in everyone's head at the same time and Marcus held a slight smirk. He is one of the only people who really understood the depth of Monique's strategic mind since he was privy to it almost daily. Monique stood and addressed the group by asking for their suggestions on how they could appear to swell their ranks without increasing their soldiers.

The ten lieutenants all had good ideas but no one could agree on anything. Although they were all capable they were more accustomed to executing plans with perfection then putting the plans together themselves. It quickly dawned on them why Monique and Dominique were in charge. Dominique and Jamal stood up with Monique and begin to lay the plan out. Monique was writing on the white board as her right hands laid it out. Dominique opened by stating that keeping minds and eyes fresh is the key. If the enemy catches you slipping they can take your product and your life.

Each crew had 20 soldiers. The soldiers would work 5 hour shifts. Jamal began to break down how the positions would fall. On these shifts one person would remain in stealth, hidden from even his crew. Two would make the transactions and two would provide protection. Each lieutenant would make the assignments based on the abilities of their people. Each lieutenant would also pick two shifts they would be stealth on as well.

The main concern as the head of the crew was getting to the money. The organized way they went about doing their job would ensure nobody caught them slipping.

Monique had organized the shift assignments on the white board so the lieutenants could make any notes they needed. The look on each man's face in the room was a cross between amazement and seriousness. Each man wanted to make sure GOD's army stayed strong. Success was how they fed their families and how they lived their lives. Many of them also felt an obligation to GOD to keep the business strong.

"Now that we have addressed your issues," Monique began to address the group, "I want all of you to retire to the dining room where I have laid out the best seafood buffet this side of the Chesapeake Bay. I appreciate everything you do and that's why we are family."

Jamal gave a slight smirk, because he knew Monique wouldn't hesitate to cancel Christmas on any one of their asses if niggas stepped out of line. It is what it is and that's the game. But he liked the twins had all of their daddy's heart and fire. They had not missed a beat in running GOD's operation. Who would have thought some bitches could be gangsta like these chicks? Jamal was smiling so hard he caught Dominique's eye.

"What the hell you doing all that grinning about Mal?"

That's what Dom called him, Mal. She knew he hated that shit, but she did it anyway.

"She thinks I won't bust her pretty little ass, but I will." Smirking he said "Go ahead with all that Mal shit Dom." Hitting her back equally with a nickname she hated. She just rolled her eyes and went to fix herself a plate before the meeting.

Jamal had wanted to fuck Dominique ever since the day he first laid eyes on her. Yeah he knows he got Shadow and everybody thinking he fucks with Dom hard like that, but truth is he hasn't gotten that far past first base with her. He didn't start off feeling about her like he does now. It actually took him awhile to accept her as an equal, but Dominique didn't ask to be taken seriously; she demanded it. After a while she put in so much work with him in the trenches he didn't have a choice but to give in. It was during one of those times in the trenches Jamal began to look at Dominique differently.

Jamal was assigned as Dominique's security detail when she was 17. He hated babysitting but also knew watching over GOD's daughters was more important than watching over his product. The twins were all GOD really cared about which made him vulnerable. His way to turn his disadvantage into a positive was to ensure the twins were well trained and well protected. Dominique was a serious girl, not into shopping sprees and hanging out at the mall. Shit, she wanted to do the things Jamal would have been doing anyway. She spent a lot of time at the shooting range, the gym and in karate. Don't get it wrong, Dominique was fine as motherfucking wine.

She was like having the best of both worlds. Her beauty was literally kissed by the sun, and her features were flawless. It didn't matter if she was wearing a pair of Diesel jeans or a Michael Kors original; she couldn't be fucked with by the average bitch. But the average nigga couldn't handle her either because she would murk his ass.

Jamal found her interesting but never said shit. They spent an enormous amount of time together and eventually began to fill comfortable enough with each other to discuss personal shit. They were coming from Karate class where Jamal had just watched Dominique put Chinese niggas on the mat. They decided to stop for dinner, it was a deviation from their normal routine and they both looked into each other's eyes knowing something was happening but unable to place it. Jamal didn't want to go anywhere fancy; he just wanted to take her someplace where she could feel regular for once. He chose Applebee's on Military Highway in Norfolk. That was so far removed from what Dominique was used to and Jamal knew she would like it.

When he pulled up into the parking lot right next to the Triple A she was all smiles. The only time Jamal saw Dominique smile is when she was about to murk somebody, "Hahahah... that shit is funny." They began to walk to the restaurant and Jamal was smiling in her face so hard he didn't see the two Lincoln Town cars pull into the parking lot but Dominique did and she pinched his arm hard; at first he didn't get it but then his sensor kicked back in and they both turned with Glocks in hand just as the shooting started.

Those niggas didn't know who they were fucking with. Dom and Mal put in work in that parking lot busting off on them niggas like it was the 4ᵗʰ of July. The sound of screeching tires made both of them fall out laughing as they watched the town cars burst out of the parking lot. When that shit was done they went into Applebee's and had the best meal they have ever had. Jamal was checking for Dom after that.

"She was made for me. But I play the back cause I don't know if she knows it." Jamal thought out loud.

Jamal was brought back to reality by someone tapping him on the shoulder. He turned around to see Dollar standing there smiling,

"What you grinning about Dollar? What's up? What you need?"

Dollar stood in Jamal's personal space, trying to piss him off, "I'm checking out the way you staring at my niece in a daze and shit, I know you want to fuck her, but she wouldn't fuck with your ole busta ass." That was all Dollar could get out before Jamal went into shut down mode. "Look Dollar you don't know what the fuck you talking about, anyway you should be in there with the other soldiers not in here fucking with me."

Dollar didn't like this smug black nigga, and when he took over Jamal was going to be one of the first to bite the dust. Dollar needed his ass right now so he would chill.

"Look Jamal I'm not trying to bust your balls, you want to fuck my niece and it's all over ya grill, but that's not why I'm here, that's your business. I need to talk to the twins."

Jamal looked Dollar up and down and thought about the many reasons why Dollar wasn't running the show with GOD away. For one he was too flamboyant, secondly he was not trustworthy, and last but definitely the most important by Jamal's standards was he was just plain stupid.

"What you want to see them for?"

"I have something important to discuss with them, but it's for their ears only. I shouldn't have to make an appointment to see my own blood."

Dollar was losing patience talking to Jamal and decided to fuck with him a little bit saying, "Does Dominique know Shadow beat your ass in his pop's shop?" Jamal looked Dollar up and down heated. Jamal had not told anyone about his confrontation with Shadow. The goons who were with him had kept it to themselves as well. They thought they would be blamed for not having Jamal's back. They thought they would be blamed for not having Jamal's back. Jamal still had plans to fuck Shadow up but family business came first.

Jamal got a sneaky grin that curled the corner of his mouth as he thought to himself; I want to see how far Dollar will go up in here. I want this pussy to jump, and he just dumb enough to do it, so I'm going to push him just a little and watch him blow.

"Look Dollar, I know you blood, but that don't mean shit, GOD set it up like this and that's the way it is."

The look Dollar had on his face let Jamal know what time it was. Dollar attempted to grab Jamal, but was a step too slow as usual and two of GOD's soldiers stepped in and grabbed him. Dollar was yelling at the top of his lungs that this was his organization and not those dyke ass bitches.

Monique and Dominique came into the room trailed closely by Marcus and members of the Hit Squad.

"What the fuck is going on in here?" Monique asked in a quiet but authoritative voice.

Dominique walked over to where Dollar was hemmed up and looked into his eyes; the look was so intense Dollar had to turn his head away. After what seemed like an hour had passed with Dominique still looking at her uncle and the room being silent, Dominique grabbed Dollar by his chin and turned him to face her. She looked into the face of the man who she had loved since she could remember. He was her daddy's little brother and Dominique couldn't understand why he was turning on her and her sister. In that instant Dominique's mind drifted to a time when her Uncle Dollar loved her unconditionally and would never think about crossing her.

Uncle Dollar was the type of Uncle every girl wanted, their daddy always did stuff with them and they never wanted for his attention. But Uncle Dollar always seemed to have time for them too. He would take the twins to the movies, parks, and shopping. You name it and they did it.

The twins felt like they had two dads and they loved the attention from both of the most important men in their lives.

Uncle Dollar knew their mom as well so the twins could get some more insight about her and just listen to stories from his perspective. Sometimes talking about Jewel made their dad sad and they hated to see the look that sometimes came over him. Uncle Dollar was always ready to share stories about Jewel.

It wasn't until the twins were grown that they realized Uncle Dollar was in love with their mother as well. It made the twins wonder if their daddy knew. Both girls also thought about how shady Uncle Dollar probably had been playing things.

Remembering her anger Dominique focused on the task at hand. Dominique squeezed her Uncle Dollar's face and yelled with hurt evident in her voice, but the danger apparent.

"That's how you feeling, fuck us huh? That's how you feeling Uncle Doll? Ok then fuck you too! Get him the fuck out of here!"

Dollar tried to say something but he was being held too tightly by the soldiers and Dominique was holding his face too tight. One of the soldiers hit him so hard in his stomach Dollar was sure something had ruptured. They dragged Dollar back to the stairs, Dollar was yelling, which was to be expected, but what he was saying is what stopped Monique in her tracks. "You bitches think you are untouchable, well get ready to get touched. I am a Dunbar baby and I am about to bring the pain to y'all asses."

Dominique wanted to kill Dollar and be done with it but Monique knew doing something like that without GOD's ok would be disastrous.

"No Dominique let him go."

One look at Dominique's face and you knew she didn't think it was a smart idea, but she understood her twin's reasoning so she fell back. The soldiers threw him down the stairs. The tumble down the stairs was rough, but on the way down Dollar made his decision. When he finally hit the bottom step he voiced out loud to himself, "Those bitches have got to go, nieces or not, they done fucked with the wrong muthafucka!"

Monique was visibly upset, she stood up and placed her hands on her waist and began to speak,

"I want every routine changed. I want all stash houses moved today. The new protocols go into place today. Dollar is family true, but I know he is about to become a problem so we need to be up on it and ready."

Dominique came to stand by Monique and then they called for Jamal and Marcus to meet them in the back conference room. When everyone was seated around the table Monique looked at Jamal with a look of concern and asked,

"What was that all about Jamal, why did he go off like that?" As much as Jamal hated to bring it to them like this, he needed to keep it real with them.

"Dollar feels he is the one that should be wearing the crown now that GOD is down not you two. He has been slipping up lately and making accusations and even trying to get some soldiers to come on his side."

Everyone at the table was silent and deep in thought, Monique spoke up first,

"He is blood, but he is a threat and will be treated as one. Dollar should not be underestimated because he knows our operation."

Marcus looked up thinking out loud "It might get ugly. "

"It already has," Dominique said as she gave Marcus a knowing look.

Marcus stood up and gave Jamal and Dominique a folder with Hit Squad 2 and Hit Squad 3 written on the covers. Marcus cleared his throat and then began

"There are 4 ex-military; some Navy seals in each of your folders. They all report to me but will be assigned to you. Their day to day operations will be at your disposal but their ultimate goal is your safety so you will follow through with what they put into place. I also want every ones main home under video surveillance and a panic room installed."

Jamal and Dominique sat up and reviewed the dossier, they knew this was serious and what this meant.

Monique slammed her fist on the table

"This is the wrong time for us to get in some shit with Uncle Dollar; we are already being challenged if not outright defiantly behind the scenes."

The mood in the room was tense, but the seriousness of what needed to be done was not lost. They knew a war was about to start, and they had to be prepared. With the new plan GOD's army was about to implement and forming Hit Squad 2 and 3 they believed they were moving in the right direction.

THE FEDS

The white van in the Hilton parking lot had a clear view of the hotel entrance. The dark tent covered up the surveillance that was going on inside. Agent Beverly and her team were hoping to get pictures of all of the major players in GOD's army. They had been tailing the "mark" for three weeks. Beverly couldn't believe he continued to work within GOD's organization after playing an instrumental role in his incarceration. Beverly shook her head and thought loyalty was so lost on the modern day criminal.

Beverly looked at her two best friends, her fellow FBI agents, and Seal team members and smiled at the things they had been through together that sealed their loyalty to one another. She called them the DP's, short for Don't Play, because that's how she felt about them, their asses don't play. Beverly reflected on the team she had chosen.

Agents Patrick and Pennington went way back to the days of Navy Special Op's with Beverly and they each brought different skills to the table that complimented each other. Agent Patrick was her electronics specialist, he could set up electronic surveillance anywhere and he always had the newest shit to use. Patrick already put a tracer on the mark's car, so they were always on point with where he was.

Beverly knew Patrick had a thing for her and that's another reason why she kept him around. His loyalty to her would definitely be needed on an operation like this.

Women thought Patrick was a nice-looking man. Beverly had watched the other female agents embarrass themselves around him. She had to admit 6'5 and 250 pounds wasn't anything to sneeze at. The man didn't have an ounce of fat on him and he was black as tar but his skin was as smooth as onyx. If she was honest with herself she would say she liked him, but she felt Agent Patrick was too needy for her. Beverly knew she probably wasn't the best person to get into a relationship with so she just let their partnership speak for itself. But anytime one of those bitches in the office got too close to him Beverly felt something in the pit of her stomach that reminded her of a menstrual cramp.

Agent Pennington was Beverly's right hand man as well as her hand to hand combat expert and recon specialist. Pennington was the shit in the Navy because he was on the boxing team and had a mean one hitter quitter. Beverly remembered seeing him put a Russian on his ass as soon as the bell sounded, the shit was awesome. Pennington was cool as shit and got along with everybody except those who decided to cross him, and then you know what they say that's your ass Mr. Postman. At 6'3 he may be smaller in stature than Patrick but his solid build and Malik Yoba looks put him on top. Because of his personality the women really acted like some damn fools around Pennington and they hated Beverly for having both men's confidence.

Both Patrick and Pennington treated Beverly somewhere between a sister and a wife. They were extremely protective of her. They both knew she had some demons that pushed her beyond her limits.

They had seen her in some very dark moods, but she was always unwilling to share what was eating her up inside. This made them both watch over her as if she was their own.

Special Agent Lucinda Beverly was a highly skilled weapons expert with looks that could kill. She was 5'6 with a little cocoa butta flavor for ya ass and diamond like eyes with lips that would make your mouth water. Her hair was dreaded up and hit the middle of her back. Beverly only let the Dominicans touch her dreads, so the shit was silky and healthy as hell. Men always look superficially when it comes to a beautiful woman. They focus on the outside beauty and booty so they miss the deadly cobra that was inside and Beverly used this to her advantage on a regular basis.

Special Agent Beverly snapped herself back to the present just as Agent Patrick loaded the facial recognition software into the Norfolk's criminal database. He was sure to get a quick identification with this. Detective Pennington scanned the perimeter and stopped on a midnight blue Hummer trying its best to look inconspicuous, but failing miserably.

"Who do we have here?", Pennington wondered out loud. Pennington took several pictures of the vehicle, but the tint on the vehicle was just as dark as what they had on the surveillance van.

Beverly noticed that Pennington appeared to have something so she maneuvered into position.

"What ya got Pen?"

Pennington was attempting to get a license plate but couldn't quite see it from his location in the van.

"That Hummer over there appears to be out here just like us. The tint is too dark to see inside and the way we are positioned I cannot see the plate."

Agent Beverly took out her binoculars and aimed them in the direction that Pennington was looking. She saw the Hummer and thought "That's a nice whip; I wonder why they are sitting on the hotel." There was no way for Beverly to see into the Hummer but she was determined to find out who was in the vehicle and why they were smack in the middle of her investigation.

"Pen I want you to make your way to the back of that Hummer without being seen and get the plate. "

The attention on the van was diverted because there was activity at the hotel entrance. The detectives saw at least fifteen people; Agent Beverly got excited and gave instructions to her crew, "Ok Patrick let's see who we got out here."

Agent Patrick began to take pictures of the crowd and feed the information into the database. As Agent Pennington prepared himself to exit the van he saw the Hummer pull out of its space and head to the back of the hotel.

"The Hummer is pulling around back, do you want me to follow it?"

Agent Beverly thought about it, "Naw maybe we are tripping, let it go. Let's continue to watch these motherfuckers. I want ID's on their vehicles, so let's get to work."

Shadow saw everyone descending from the Airport Hilton and noticed the level of security around the twins appeared to be beefed up. Shadow wondered who all of these new diesel looking motherfuckers were. Dominique was surrounded by three dudes Shadow had never laid eyes on, but if he had to guess he would say they were professionals. That's when Shadow knew something big must be up because Dominique could handle her damn self and she sure as hell don't like help. He noticed a small gap between Dominique's guards and her; he was just able to catch the look on her face. It was somewhere between annoyance and danger. Shadow had witnessed the danger look before.

Before Shadow could ponder anymore on why they were are all meeting up here like this, he felt his phone vibrate against his waist. A quick peek at the display brought a scowl to his face as he noticed Dollar's number. He answered the phone sounding irritate, "What?"

Dollar was out of breath and mad at the world. He couldn't believe the twins had the nerve to play him like that. He didn't give a fuck who they thought they were he was Dollar mutherfucking Bill and bitches better recognize. Dollar felt as though the twins should just turn the business over to him just because.

But now he realized he was going to have to take it from them by force. Dollar heard the attitude in Shadow's voice and wondered what the fuck his problem was.

"Yo Shadow where you at? I need you to come get me right now man, these bitches got me fucked up."

Shadow looked at the phone like it was speaking in a different language because Dollar didn't sound like himself. He was coughing and groaning like he was in some kind of pain.

"I'm right outside of the Airport Hilton watching the twins."

Dollar tried to sit up, but his side hurt badly from the fall but he did manage to hold on to a railing and pull himself up. "Bitches" was all he could say. "Ok come to the back of the hotel I am at the railing and I need help."

Shadow just shook his head because he knew then Dollar had let his mouth cash a check and he had non-sufficient funds to cover it. Shadow thought back to when he first started fucking with Dollar, he was writing bad ass whopping checks then too.

Shadow was chilling at the Shop-N-Go located in the Brambelton section of Norfolk watching Dollar Bill in an altercation with a small time dealer about money owed to him. Everybody knew who Dollar was, they knew he was GOD's blood, but he carried shit differently than GOD. Dollar was sloppy and grimier with his shit.

*Now don't get it wrong, GOD would peel your cap if
need be, but best believe you deserved it. Dollar was
always fucking with somebody for no reason. Really
niggas were fed up with Dollar and were about to send a
message to his ass. In the hood it's not like no Mafioso
shit where you had to get permission to peel a nigga cap.
No one wanted to step on GOD's toes and this is why
they had allowed Dollar to terrorize the area for so long;
but enough was enough.*

*The Brambelton niggas were about to put in work
four deep on Dollar's ass, but for reasons he couldn't
even understand Shadow wasn't feeling that shit. Where
he came from real niggas stated their beef and handled
that shit like men. Shadow couldn't stomach this four on
one shit that was about to jump off. At the same time,
Shadow was not checking for Dollar's ass either. He
knew the ass whopping Dollar was about to get was one
that was well deserved.*

*Shadow grew up with the Dunbar clan and he
knew how fucked up Dollar could be. Shadow felt a
certain amount of loyalty to the family but he wasn't
going to put himself out but so far for some of Dollar's
bullshit. He pulled his gun on 3 niggas and told Dollar
to handle his business with them one at a time or bounce.
Dollar knew he couldn't go out like no punk so he
commenced to whipping each one of their asses
individually. Shadow couldn't believe Dollar was kind of
good with his hands, although dumb as a brick for
walking into niggas territory popping shit by himself.
Dollar was so used to living off his brother's rep that he
never spotted the signs of danger.*

After shit settled down, Dollar told Shadow he was in the midst of doing his own shit. He said he was breaking off from his brother and he wanted him to work for him, be his protection, his right hand. Shadow was skeptical that Dollar could be the boss of a dog let alone a crime family. He lacked qualities that made men want to follow you over a cliff. His business sense was uncertain, and his common sense was dubious at best. Shadow informed Dollar Bill he was his own man and didn't work for a crew, but he freelanced and would be available to hire for specific jobs.

Shadow laughed when he thought about how he first got mixed up with this clown. When he pulled to the back of the hotel he could see Dollar stumble out of the alley and make his way to the waiting truck looking like he got the shit beat out of him.

"What the fuck you get yourself into Dollar?"

Dollar had a sinister smile on his face that also looked pained,

"I'm going to kill those bitches and that hoe ass nigga Jamal. Time to step up our game Shadow."

Shadow gave Dollar a look like he had lost his damn mind. He didn't know what the fuck Dollar meant by it was time for them to step up their game. He was there to do a job; not to be involved in any takeover. Shadow was now having second thoughts about even being involved thinking, *"This shit is going too far."* He pulled out of the parking lot with a lot on his mind and some big decisions to make.

QUESTIONS

Jury selection on God's trial took place last week and GOD had a good feeling about the progress Tonya was making with his case. He was more concerned with what was happening on the outside with his organization. He wanted to be more accessible to his girls just in case they needed him. GOD knew Monique was more than capable of handling business and Dominique would keep niggas in line, but he knew it took a lot of balls to come after him. He still had questions that were not answered, like who is the informant in his crew and why the fuck does Special Agent Beverly want to fuck him over so bad? That last question made GOD smile, he kind of liked the girl, liked her spunk and her courage. But like or not, she was about to get dealt with.

GOD decided to call his main man Michael so he picked up the phone after pushing all the other inmates to the back and placed the call. GOD couldn't help but smile as he waited for Michael to answer the phone. They grew up together and were as tight as brothers. Michael didn't enter the same business as GOD; actually he went the exact opposite. Michael joined the Navy and retired as a Captain. His only child Marcus followed his footsteps by joining the Navy and took advantage of everything the navy had to offer. The nasal sounding operator interrupted his thoughts as he heard his best friend's voice come through the line.

"Yes I will accept the charges. What up Bro?"

"Mike, what's good fam? Everything is lovely."

This was the way old friends talked in code. Everything is lovely is an answer that means GOD's baby girls are good. GOD knows Marcus is watching over Monique. Marcus thinks GOD doesn't know he is love with his baby girl, but he does, and he wouldn't have it any other way. Michael felt the same way. The same with Jamal, he came to visit GOD shortly after he got to jail and confessed his love for Dominique and promised to protect her with his life. Knowing both of his ladies had real niggas watching their back made GOD's time more bearable.

"How is business Michael?"

"Well you know me Bro, I can't complain." This was another code for Michael to reassure GOD Monique was still handling business like a pro.

"What's shaking with them cats around the way?" Code for asking what the streets are up to.

Michael quickly replied "Foul." So GOD knew a war was imminent.

"Word to my first." And with that Michael knew to let Monique know her father wanted to see her. They said their goodbyes and GOD went back to his cell to think of how he might be useful to his girls.

Lock down can be hard and Northern Neck Regional Jail was no different. GOD was hearing good things about his chances at trial and was hopeful.

The next day the CO came for GOD to tell him he had an attorney visit. He knew exactly who it was, his first born. When he made it to the attorney room he could see her silhouette standing with her arms folded by the window. The CO took the handcuffs off and left the room.

"Hello baby girl."

Monique felt a sense of warm cover her heart and she turned around to get her fill of the man she loved most in this world.

"Hi Poppa, I miss you so much."

"Come sit down baby and talk to your poppa. We got plenty of time to talk shop. Tell me what's new with you." They both moved towards the table and chairs to have a seat. Monique reached across the table and grabbed her poppa's hands and said,

"Oh Poppa, you have not changed a bit, you always wanted to know what was up with me."

GOD could see Monique's eyes light up and he knew why. He sat back and let his baby girl talk to him.

"Poppa I think I am in love, but I don't know what to do with it. I don't want to open my heart to Marcus and lose him."

The look on GOD's face was one of confusion, he hoped Marcus was doing right by his baby girl, but he kept his thoughts to himself and asked instead,

"Why would you lose him baby girl? That boy is crazy about you, always has been always will be." GOD reached across the table and grabbed his first born's hands again.

Monique's eyes dropped to the floor and a tear crept from her eyes. Monique would never let another person outside of Dominique see her vulnerable.

"I just keep thinking about how you lost momma and what effect that had on your heart, I don't know if I am strong enough to stand that."

It hurt God to see his precious baby cry but he let her get it out.

"Give love a chance, give Marcus a chance. That man loves you girl. I trust him and I know he will protect you with his life. You listening baby?"

"Yes Daddy I am."

Monique only called him daddy when she was scared, other than that she called him poppa. So he knew she was really struggling with what to do. God decided he would leave her with her thoughts on the matter so he changed the subject.

"What's going on in the streets baby girl?"

Monique knew what he was doing, and she knew why, but Monique also knew she needed distracting.

"Poppa, Uncle Dollar is out of control, he is coming after Dominique and me because he wants to run the empire."

GOD always knew his little brother was ambitious, but also stupid. He didn't want to believe Dollar would go against blood, but GOD also knew money, power, and respect would make a man turn on his own momma. The room was silent as he thought about what his daughter was telling him.

GOD always knew Dollar would do anybody dirty including him. Dollar didn't know the only reason that GOD kept him around is out of respect for Poppa Dunbar. Dunbar wanted his boys to be close, wanted them to have each other's back by all means necessary. There were some issues between Pops Dunbar and his youngest brother Dro that he didn't want to see GOD and Dollar go through. But he also knew Dollar was so jealous of his older brother that if he wasn't watched closely he would be the one to hurt him.

Poppa Dunbar made his oldest son promise to make Dollar a necessary part of the family operation so he would feel that he was his own man, just like his big brother. GOD never liked the idea, but how could he tell his father no? This man had taught him everything he knew about being a man, about family, and about life. For Poppa Dunbar, the man who has held his mother down and never mistreated her, GOD would make this sacrifice. But deep down inside he knew that one day he was going to have to check Dollar, and when that day came GOD knew it would break his poppa's heart.

Monique raised her voice and called her dads name again, he had a far off look in his eyes like he was in a different place and time. GOD looked into Monique's eyes and said,

"Your uncle is nursing a big hate. He assumed too much. Dollar is a fool if he thinks he can go against me locked up or not. But I don't want any of you to sleep on him, because I trained him just like I trained you. He just doesn't apply it as well as you girls do but he knows it so don't lower your guard."

Monique listened to her daddy because she knew he was talking things that would mean life or death.

"I really wish it didn't have to be like this, Uncle Dollar could be an asset to the family, but he doesn't want to roll with it, he wants to buck the system, so he got to get it. But I wanted to talk to you first Poppa. Dominique was about to rock his ass to sleep yesterday."

GOD shook his head as a deep laugh grew from the pit of his belly "Dominique is that bitch for sho, her and her Uncle Dollar were always so close, so I know he must have really stepped in it."

"Show me the plan. "

Monique pulled a dossier out of her Coach briefcase and showed it to her poppa. After reading about the surveillance to be placed on not only Dollar but all of the large buyers in the area and the plans for GOD's army and the Hit Squads he looked up from the dossier with a bright smile on his face. Seeing him smile at the decisions she had made had Monique feeling giddy inside like a little kid.

"This is perfect baby girl; exactly what I would hope to have come up with."

GOD was smiling at his first born while he continued to hold the dossier in his hands. Monique was shaking her head up and down loving her father's approval.

"I know poppa, I have been taught by the best. I have gone through every scenario and I have brought Dominique and Jamal up to date and given them their assignments. They each have 5 lieutenants under them and will make sure our shit is tight."

Monique and her father talked about the streets for a little while longer and then alarms blared through the speakers.

"Fuck it's a lock down baby, you stay here, they will be here to get me I'm sure."

Just as GOD made that statement the door pushed open and Dollar walked in.

"What the fuck," was all Dollar got out before GOD was across the table with his hand around Dollar's throat. Gone was his normal cool demeanor. He was trying to crush his little brother's larynx.

"You threaten my blood nigga... You hoe ass nigga you better back the fuck down today or I will forget we have the same parents!"

Dollar could barely keep his eyes from rolling to the back of his head. The deputies pulled GOD off of him, but they were not aggressive, they just didn't want a dead visitor on their hands.

"Alright I'm good; get your fucking hands off of me." GOD stated sternly enough for the deputies to know he wasn't fucking with them.

Dollar finally caught his breath enough to notice the occupants of the room. He looked Monique in her eyes; the heat radiating from him said it all, it was on and popping. Dollar had made a special trip to the prison to speak to his brother man to man. He knew the easiest way to get to the top was to get GOD to sanction it. Dollar honestly felt maybe GOD wasn't aware he wanted the position and all he needed to do was speak with him and that would be that.

"What the fuck is she doing here?" Dollar shot Monique another look.

GOD looked at the way the deputies were looking at Monique and did some fast thinking before Dollar's stupid ass blew her cover. He turned to Monique and said,

"Let's finish this another day and I look forward to hearing more about the trial, tell Ms. Green I need to see her tomorrow."

Monique took the hint, gathered her things and left the room with a deputy escort. The other deputy addressed GOD "The alarm was a false alarm. You have twenty minutes with your visitor but I will be right outside so please don't kill each other." With that he left the room closing the door behind him.

GOD turned his attention back to Dollar. He was using every muscle in his body not to wrap his large hands around his brother's throat again.

"What the fuck are you doing Larry?"

Larry stood close to the door and stared at his older brother. He knew GOD was one step from trying to make a move on him again and he was going to avoid that.

"Lawrence I am sorry, but I really needed to see you."

Dollar and GOD always called each other by their real names when they were alone.

"What the fuck are you doing threatening my seeds man, what the fuck is wrong with you?"

The look Dollar had on his face told GOD he was going to make this hard. Dollar looked his brother straight in his face and asked him to let him run the business until he beat his charges.

"Come on Lawrence you know this is how it is supposed to be, them bitc...," Catching himself he continued "I mean my nieces are not equipped to run this shit like I am."

God rubbed his temples because his younger brother could really miss him with all of this stupid shit he was talking.

"Look the twins have been groomed for this since the day they were born, this is no different than if I would have had twin boys, they would have taken over, not you, so why are you sweating what decisions I have made about how I run my business?"

Dollar looked at his big brother or rather through him because he couldn't believe what he was hearing.

"Do you mean you are really going to trust them to keep the family business at the level you had it? Man you are really fucked up. Ok well you had your chance to make this right."

With that Dollar stretched his 6'4 frame and shook his head back and forth. He was just as tall as his older brother but he didn't carry his frame with the same dignity that GOD did.

"I'm out!"

Dollar stared at his brother hoping again he would change his mind. But GOD stood up and said,

"Then step, but if you don't back down, I'm going to let them lay you down."

With that the brothers knew they could never go back to what it was. They could never be the illusion of sibling bliss again. Dollar banged on the window and yelled for the deputy, he turned around and looked at his brother.

"I hope you rot in here, and them bitch ass nieces of mine, I might fuck them both before I kill them!" with that Dollar slipped out of the door and out of GOD's reach.

GOD shook his head and said a silent good bye to his brother. He would allow Dominique to rock his ass, but thought,

"What the fuck am I going tell my poppa? Shit!"

DOLLAR BILL

Once he left the prison Dollar jumped into the passenger seat of his black Dodge Magnum SE. Shadow was driving and one look at his face told him pretty much all he needed to know, shit was about to blow.

"So what you going do next?" Shadow couldn't help but break the silence. He might as well use this ride back to Norfolk to get a better understanding of what this nigga was up to and decide whether or not to stop fucking with him.

Dollar shook his head with thoughts of what he was going tell his momma spinning in his head.

"I got to kill my blood and although them muthafuckas deserve it for disrespecting me, I still feel a certain kind a way about it."

Shadow understood what Dollar was saying, but Shadow also knew Dollar was thinking about the fact that he was about to take on GOD. Shit, truth be told Shadow was questioning why he was on this side of the gun himself; but a job is a job or was it more than that? Had Shadow allowed a personal grudge and a deep seeded unfulfilled lust to fuck his judgment up? Those thoughts continued to linger as the ride fell silent.

As they rode on in silence Tupac's Dear Momma played low in the background and Dollar looked out the window and thought about how close him and his big brother used to be.

Truth be told, and Dollar wouldn't admit this to anybody else, he admired his brother, always had. Lawrence had everything Dollar didn't. His brother had swag, he walked it; he dressed it, and he looked it. Don't get it wrong, Dollar also inherited the smooth dark skin and 6'4 frame that was a Dunbar man trait. Poppa Dunbar used to tell his boys that Dunbar men could make a woman cream in her panties just by walking into the room. Dollar just couldn't carry it as well as GOD no matter how hard he tried.

They were only three years apart, but everything always came easy to GOD and Dollar felt he had to work hard for it all. Despite all that, Dollar and GOD were inseparable when they were young. Dollar wanted to be just like him. When GOD returned from studying law at William and Mary University in Williamsburg he brought with him a coke connect that would put the family at the top of the drug game in Virginia. Dollar noticed a change in GOD's attitude. He couldn't put his finger on it exactly but didn't focus on it too long because GOD gave Dollar a large role in the organization. Dollar recalled the original set up of the organization which had him as second in charge. He had the business growing and running smoothly. Two things happened that changed the foundation of Dollar's world. One Poppa Dunbar was diagnosed with pancreatic cancer. Poppa was the glue that held GOD and Dollar so tightly together. With Poppa Dunbar extremely sick GOD could more clearly see Dollar's slick and conniving ways. Poppa Dunbar was no longer there to run the interference Dollar needed to eventually take over the family business.

The second and probably most devastating to both brothers was the death of Jewel. Jewel was the light in GOD's eyes and when she died a part of GOD died as well. The only room left in his heart was for the twin girls Jewel died giving birth to. No one noticed how Jewel's death affected Dollar; but why should they he wasn't her husband. Everyone thought him to be in the background, but what they didn't know is Dollar was secretly in love with Jewel and had always resented that she chose GOD over him.

Jewel always thought of Dollar as the little brother she never had, but his feelings for her ran much deeper than that. It cut deep in his soul when she died. Dollar always believed she would eventually be his. After these tragedies GOD scaled back on the responsibilities he gave to Dollar. The duties had now been secretly reassigned to Michael GOD's best friend. Secretly, because Michael was the head of the Navy Seals division located in Norfolk, Virginia. GOD didn't think Dollar knew Michael was making decisions, but he knew and it pissed him off. He would bide his time, build his network, and eventually take over what he felt was the family business.

The car coming to an abrupt stop brought Dollar back to the present and all of the stress was building up in his head for the battles to come.

"Where the fuck are we?" Dollar asked Shadow who had his eyes glued to all the traffic ahead.

"We are in Portsmouth stuck at this damn tunnel, I don't care when I come through this muthafucka it's always backed up."

Dollar sat up in his seat and stretched and yawned loudly.

"Damn we got here quick." He said looking out the window.

"No man, you just been on some zombie shit for a minute, I done stopped for gas and everything and you didn't blink." Shadow chuckled lightly.

Dollar shook his head, because he knew Shadow was looking at his ass sideways.

"I got a lot of shit on my mind man."

The look Shadow gave him confirmed what Dollar was thinking, but Shadow wouldn't verbalize his thoughts he just said,

"I understand; you done declared war on your family, so what's your plan?"

Dollar always dreamed about being in a situation to take over the family from his older brother, but now the reality of having to actually put his thoughts into a full action plan was weighing down on him. Dollar hoped GOD would have enough loyalty to him to just turn things over without having to go all out, but things didn't quite work out like that.

"First thing I got to do is disrupt their cash flow, with some simultaneous raids and stick ups."

Dollar's eyes began to get small as his conniving ways began to take form.

"Then follow that by taking out the most ruthless of the twins, Dominique. Let's see if that will make the rest of them rethink their position."

Shadow sat there looking at Dollar as he discussed his play and immediately saw the holes in the plan and since his life would be on the line as well if he decided to roll with him he had to speak on it.

"And just what are the twins and GOD's army supposed to be doing while you are running through they shit...playing spades, drinking? What?"

Dollar knew where Shadow was coming from, he had his own misgivings as well, but he knew he could pull this off.

"This is why it has to be planned out and executed flawlessly." Dollar tried to sound confident while he said it but his facial expression didn't lie, it showed the weight of his decisions.

Shadow was not convinced, and he knew he needed to get some perspective. He needed to talk to his pops. Everybody called him Big Rolla because he would roll up on your ass quick and bust a cap in it. It's where Shadow got his kill game from and he was the only one Shadow trusted to keep shit 100.

Dollar noticed the skeptical look on Shadow's face and wondered if Shadow was going ride with him on this.

"What's on your mind Shadow?"

The gruff sound coming from Dollar shattered the silence and the men looked each other in the eye with different feelings running through their heads. Shadow was the first to break the intense stare but he couldn't share the full weight of his thoughts. Instead he said,

"I'm good Dollar, just got heavy shit on my mind."

Dollar knew it was bullshit, but decided to let it ride for now because he had his own heavy shit to deal with.

"Yes!" Shadow yelled as he hit the steering wheel, "Fucking traffic is moving now! I bet there wasn't shit going on to have this shit backed up like this."

Shadow was able to make it to Chesapeake in record time. He dropped Dollar off at his 4 bedroom 2 ½ bath condo in the Greenbrier section and they agreed to have a planning session the next day. Shadow made a bee line for the Green Run section of Virginia Beach with one thing on his mind; to talk at his pops.

BIG ROLLA/SHADOW

Big Rolla sat in his office at his Killa Kuts Barber shop and thought about the news he had just received. Word had already made it back to him that Dollar was declaring war on the twins. Big Rolla of all people knew Dominique would be on the war path and would not stop until her Uncle Dollar was put in the ground. Rolla sighed as he thought about how this must be affecting his old friend. Surely giving the okay for his seeds to take out his baby brother couldn't have been an easy decision to make. "It's just the hustla mentality they were raised with, you don't fuck with us."

Rolla always considered himself a hustla and a scholar. He didn't sell drugs; that wasn't his hustle. He could have inherited a drug empire if that's what he wanted but Rolla was his own man; been that way since he saw his father gunned down and his mother raped when he was 10 years old. A pain surfaced in his heart as he reminisced about his father and the tragedy that changed the course of his young life.

Big Rolla's father, Dr. J. as everyone called him since his ball playing days was a pimp and a hustler. His murder was payback and the rape of his mother was what it was, made to humiliate. The killer never knew Shannon, later known as Big Rolla was in the house. His mother heard the commotion in the home and the first thing she did was hide Shannon in the cut out hole in the closet that Dr. J made to hide things.

Shannon remembered wishing his mother would hide with him. The last thing she said to Shannon was

"Don't come out of here until one of use comes and get you. I don't care what you hear!"

Shannon knew things were about to get bad, he did what his mom said, just like his dad told him to always do, he stayed put. Shannon heard the screaming and hollering in his house then he heard the gun shots. They sounded like sonic booms to his young ears, but he was from the hood so he knew what time it was. The screaming he heard from his mother was what brought him out of his hiding place.

Shannon made his way to his secret passage in his house he made so he could be nosey; he knew no one would see him. What he saw turned his young heart cold and tore his world apart. Shannon saw his pops, Dr. J to all, but to him he was the man who he admired beyond reason, with a knife sticking out of his right eye. All you could see was the pearl handle with a dragon design on it, that's how deep it was in his pops eye. Shannon's eyes grew real big when he thought he could see clear through his dad's chest. His dad was gone and Shannon couldn't breathe, it wasn't until he heard his mom scream again he came back to the present.

He refocused his eyes and noticed there was a really big man fucking his mother in her ass. The man had his beautiful mother bent over the couch and was pumping into her back with all of his might, his mother was screaming so loudly it pierced young Shannon's ear. Shannon saw the man punch his mother in her neck and yell at her to shut the fuck up.

"You like this big dick in your ass don't you? I've been wanting to fuck this big ass for years. You wouldn't give it to nobody but that bitch ass nigga, now look at him, and now look at you. My dick to the hilt in this ass, fuck you bitch!"

He punched her in her neck again damn near knocking her out. But Shannon knew she was still with him because he could hear her crying. What he heard next shook Shannon to his knees. His mother's voice was cracking and barely audible, but she could be heard saying,

"He was your brother Sam, why would you do that to your brother? Oh my God! Stop you're hurting meeeeeeeee..."

Shannon couldn't believe the man whose back was to him was his Uncle Sam. He couldn't believe he had killed his pops and was raping his mother. Shannon made his way to the stash spot his pops didn't think he knew about. This is where his dad kept his weapons, money and his drugs.

"There it is." Shannon picked up his pops Sig Sauer P229 semi-automatic. Dr. J didn't let Shannon shoot much but he was teaching him. Shannon knew enough to help his mom.

Shannon could still hear his mom and was determined to end what she was going through. His stomach was hurting but he refused to cry. Shannon remembered his pops said that "Crying is for suckas and I ain't raising no suckas."

Shannon was determined to put something in the ground. He crept into the living room, the closer he got, the more he wanted his pops just to get up from the chair and beat the shit out of his uncle.

"But pops ain't never getting up again, he through and Uncle Sam is a bitch and I'm all my momma got."

Shannon yelled at the top of his lungs with more fear or anger than he could ever remember having in his young life.

"Get the fuck off my momma you bitch ass nigga." Shannon gave his best impression of his pop with his heart beating like a bongo drum in his chest.

Sam turned his head real quick, never taking his dick out. Taking in his nephew and despite the rage he was sure was boiling in the young boy; Sam could smell the fear as it reeked from his pores.

"Well what do we have here?" He continued to pump his dick viciously into the ass in front of him "Check my nephew out. Yeah you a trooper just like us boy. I see you got your Sauer. What the .fuck you going to do wit that?" Sam continued pumping his dick in and out of Shannon's mom turning his back on Shannon, wrong move. Shannon aimed like his pops had taught him and fired without another thought. The scream coming from his mom was deafening, he watched her jump up from the couch with brain matter rolling down

*her back. She ran to her husband and saw there was
nothing else she could do for him. Shannon could tell
she wanted to break down, but what he saw gave him a
new respect for his mom. She walked over to her son,
kissed him on his lips and told him to go pack up the shit
out of his dad's special closet. Shannon knew enough to
know in this lifestyle you couldn't sit around and wait on
the cops. He ran off to do exactly what his momma told
him to do, just like his daddy taught him. When he
returned his mom had already packed up their clothes
and they bounced in his father's Cadillac, leaving
Norfolk and heading down to Charlotte, NC.*

*Pushing the large car down the road and
fumbling for a cigarette with shaking hands, his mother
began to talk to him "Son what your uncle did was
fucked up, he was wrong, but you can believe Snake sent
him." Snake was his father's competition and his
mother's former boyfriend. His father had snatched his
mom from Snake years ago and made her the queen of
his empire. Snake had held a deadly grudge ever since.
"Snake is going to keep coming until he kills us both. He
knows you are going to grow up and he knows you will
want revenge. I'm going to take you to my brother, he
will train you, make sure you are tight, make you the
killer you need to be in order to stay alive in this world.
I didn't want this life for you, but you are not going to be
able to live the square life that you deserve until Snake is
dead. Do you understand me baby?"*

*Shannon sat in the back seat of the large vehicle and
silently grieved for his father. He would miss him so
much and no one had the right to take him away.*

Shannon was taking it all in. He knew his momma was thinking just like pops had taught her to do; and if they were going to his Uncle Onion house then pops had already put this into place.

Shannon knew he was just carrying out what his pops had already set in motion so he looked at his momma and said,

"I understand everything you saying Momma and on my word Snake's days are numbered."

The look on his momma face switched from worry to pride and they rode in silence. From that day forward Shannon learned everything associated with killing and making a nigga disappear. He stayed in NC for 8 years until he left for William and Mary University in Williamsburg, Virginia.

Being in Williamsburg brought his mission to put that nigga Snake to sleep in full swing. Shannon figured all he had to do was go to Norfolk and split Snake's wig and hop back on Interstate 264 and make it back to Williamsburg without being noticed. The whole thing should only take 2 hours. Shannon's roommate was a Norfolk cat who had all the ladies locked down on campus. The roommates were inseparable; they clicked right from the start. William and Mary wasn't known for its diversity so having somebody to really relate to on campus was just what both boys needed.

The boys began to confide in each other about everything including Shannon's pop's death. The pain inside of Shannon was as strong as if he was still 10 years old.

Any other boy would have never been able to grow into a man of substance, but Shannon's mom wasn't having it. She made sure he was a deadly machine and top of his class. The look on Shannon's roommate's face when he told him about that night was comforting. He looked as though he wanted to blast on the next nigga that said the wrong shit. Shannon felt like this was how close he would feel to a brother if he ever had one.

"So when we going to bust on this nigga Shan?" was the words that came out of his roommates mouth.

Those few words formed a bond between Shannon and his roommate Lawrence. They planned the death of Snake like it was a final exam and carried it out like graduation was near. By the end of their time at W&M Shannon had introduced Lawrence to his family which turned out to be the biggest drug connect on the east coast. The family was impressed with Lawrence and decided to front him the coke to start his empire; a relationship that has endured for over twenty years.

Thinking about that time in his life always gave Rolla mixed feelings, he knew his life didn't float the exact way he would have liked it to, and he knew his pop's death had changed the course but at the end of the day he had risen to the top. Big Rolla did pick up a hustle that became invaluable to his college roommate who took his connect back to Norfolk and changed the game. His roommate put so much work in on the streets of the Hampton Roads area that people began to call him GOD. What no one knew of was the bond between GOD and Rolla and they chose to keep it that way.

Rolla's hustle was making people disappear. After he received his degree in Bio-Chemistry Rolla joined the Navy where he became a strategist. He also was putting in work for GOD; knocking off those who crossed him or tried to become competition; they would simply disappear. But that was in the past. Once Rolla got married and had Jr. he put a muzzle on "the life".

Rolla remembered what not getting out of "the life" cost him and his family with his father's murder. Rolla now owned a string of barbershops called Killa Kuts but every now and then he got rid of a problem. And a problem is what he knew his son Jr. was bringing to him; he could tell just by the wavy lines on his son's forehead. Shadow had entered Killa Kuts and spoke to the barbers and customers before making it to his father's office. What he didn't know, couldn't know was Rolla saw him coming before he even turned on the block. Rolla had surveillance cameras on every block leading up to his business that fed into a state of the art security system. Rolla had made many a man disappear in the past easily because of their lack of surveillance. So when Jr., or Shadow, as all of his friends called him made his way upstairs to his pop's office Rolla was ready to give him his full attention.

Shadow walked over and gave his father a manly hug and pound. Shadow was always amazed every time he was in his dad's presence at how poised and strong he always appeared to be. Shadow was in awe of his dad and respected his insight.

"Hey pops, I need to rap with you about some stuff. Do you have a minute for your favorite kid?"

Rolla laughed that laugh that always reminded Shadow of Eddie Murphy.

"Favorite kid, hell you my only kid so I guess you might as well be my favorite."

Father and son had this back and forth every time they got together. Shadow always wanted a brother or sister, but Rolla would joke and say then who would be the favorite kid.

Rolla put his hand out telling his son to sit on the couch while he went to the fully stocked bar and pored them both a Hennessey and Coke.

"Here drink this and tell me what's up"

Shadow took the drink from his dad, turned the glass to his lips and in one swift movement the drink disappeared.

"Thanks pops, I needed that. Pops I think I fucked up, I broke one of your rules. Never get involved in another man's beef."

The left eyebrow on Rolla's face turned up but he didn't speak; he allowed his son to get it all out and then he would kick knowledge to him. Shadow placed his hands under his chin,

"Pops I been freelancing for a while, I really don't want to be associated with any crew, but I might have got sucked into a beef between Dollar and GOD."

Now Rolla's other eyebrow was raised. He had recently gotten word GOD wanted him to come to the jail; he wondered what it was about and now he knew. Rolla had heard enough so he threw his hands up to get his son's attention.

"Have you completed the job you were hired to do son?"

Shadow walked over to the floor to ceiling window in the spacious office that took up the entire top floor of Killa Kuts.

"No Pops I have been tailing Dominique and I can pick her off at any time because she has no clue I'm on her."

Rolla shook his head as he put his large basketball player hands on his head he thought, *"I taught him all I know and he still can't see when his tail is busted."*

"At some point your tail was picked up son"

Shadow turned around from the window so fast his whole body sounded like it cracked.

"No way pops, how you figure that?"

Rolla went on to explain to his son that his presence has been requested to come to the jail by GOD and the only reason could be to discuss him and his actions. Shadow stared straight ahead and what was in his eyes wasn't fright; the look was more like concern. He didn't want to get his pops caught up in anything.

"Look pops I'm not trying to get you caught up in none of my bullshit. I know you and GOD go way back."

Rolla put his hands up and Shadow knew that meant to shut up and let his pops talk.

"Son I don't understand why you are mixed up with Dollar's stupid ass. He been trying to be GOD since they were kids. How you roll is up to you... don't worry about me, GOD and I will be ok. But getting involved needs to be about you... not bitch ass Dollar!"

Shadow sat quietly as he let what his father said sink in. He noticed his father had raised his voice which he rarely did. Shannon was so deep in thought he didn't notice the look of regret in his father's eyes.

"Pop I don't know what I'm going to do, it's complicated. I got mixed feelings about Dollar's motives and I have personal reasons to stay close to the situation, I just don't know."

Shadow shook his head as he began to put things in perspective, which he always was able to do when he talked to his pops. He went back to sit on the couch and looked deep into his pop's eyes,

"What are you going to do about GOD?"

Surprisingly to Shannon Rolla smiled, "I'm going to roll up to Northern Neck Regional Jail tomorrow and go see my stick man. Everything will be good no matter what you decide to do. What you need to be is ready to live with your decisions ok?"

What his father was saying to him began to sink in. If you were going to play in this man's game than you better be ready to be a man.

"Yeah pops I understand. I'm about to bounce, I got to go see ma and make some other runs."

They both stood up. Rolla was always amazed his son, the little boy who used to climb on his back, was now looking his own 6'4 frame dead in the eye. He had mixed feelings about Jr. being in the business, but he also knew he had to let him make his own decisions and mistakes. All he could do was be there to offer counsel when he needed it.

"That's right, go check on your ma so she can stop plucking my nerves."

The men hugged. Rolla held on a little longer than normal and Shadow noticed it. Shadow began to have thoughts about how his pops must really feel about him being in this line of work especially when he didn't have to be.

TURMOIL

There was a lot going on in the family right now. Someone in the family was snitching, Uncle Dollar was tripping, money was still on point but niggas in the street were looking thirsty. Dominique sat in her plush living room in the Shadow Land Estate section of Virginia Beach. She began to think about all the payback she needed to deal with in the name of her father and in the name of the family.

"I am not finished either. I need to step to this bitch ass Special Agent, get to some of these jury members and find out who the fuck is snitching."

Dominique began to relax and enjoy her home. She came to this house when she wanted to get away and think. The only person who knew about this home was her sister and now Hit Squad 3. Jamal didn't even know about this spot. Her living room color scheme was meant to comfort. A deep tan sectional with plush tan and black pillows surrounded a stone fireplace Dominique used every time she came despite the season. The carpet was Burberry plush, cream with faint black speckles. Dominique liked how her feet sunk into the carpet when she walked. On this day she relaxed on her sectional with a glass of champagne and began her planning phase for Agent Beverly.

"This chick knows too much and I want to know how. There is no way she could arrest my daddy without help; where did that help come from? Well you know what; I'm just going to have to ask her."

Dominique spent the remainder of the day on her plan until she fell asleep. She was awakened some hours later by her cell phone.

"Who dis?" a groggy Dominique answered pissed that her sleep was disturbed.

There was silence on the other end of the phone to the normal ear, but Dominique could hear someone breathing. She checked the caller ID and noticed the number was blocked. This might have scared the average chick, but not Dominique. In the most self-assured tone she could muster she stated, "Let me know when you ready to play with a real bitch."

She hung up the phone. Dominique knew she should report the phone call to the Hit Squad, but she also knew she could handle anything that came her way. Refreshed and with a plan Dominique changed into her stalking clothes, black True Religion jeans, a black Gucci sweater, and a black handled Glock. She went to her underground garage and selected a simple black Lexus. It was time to set a mouse trap and catch the Big Cheese.

Dominique noticed Desmond one of the members of her Hit Squad in the cut and figured she better take him with her rather than him following her and blowing up her spot. As she approached Desmond she noticed how thick and handsome he was. She didn't normally go for the bald headed brothers but Desmond possessed a presence that made her wonder what he was thinking. Desmond had Dennis Haysbert looks with a NFL player's body standing 6'6 with too much thickness to go around; but that's not what had Dominique's attention.

Whatever it was she decided to push it to the back and pay attention to the duty at hand.

"Desmond I got to do some recon, I figured you could roll with me rather than tailing me."

The smile that came across his face was unexpected and the deep baritone that escaped his lips sent a chill down her neck

"I agree, I need to keep you close because you a pistol for real."

Desmond ended with a wink and hopped in her car. The rest of Dominique's Hit Squad was ordered to stay back. They rode in silence with each taking turns checking the other out. The sexual tension was apparent and she didn't quite know what to do with it. Everyone assumed that she was involved with Jamal and although she was attracted to him their relationship never progressed and Dominique couldn't quite put her finger on the reason. But she knew that she was very particular about who she let share her bed; she preferred a boss or at least boss material.

Dominique made a turn at the Corporate Blvd light off of Military Highway and parked in the parking lot of the Water's Edge apartment complex. She noticed how pretty these apartments were. The sign located at the entrance boasted that the Water's Edge Apartments offered spacious 1 and 2 bedroom apartment homes with washer and dryer included. Dominique wasn't in the market for an apartment but the building to the left of the

Water's Edge Apartments was the Norfolk Division of the FBI. Desmond followed her gaze through her binoculars and recognized where they were. He smiled inside recognizing this vixen's skill.

Dominique's research told her that the Norfolk field office was under the leadership of Special Agent in Charge John Bowser and Assistant Special Agents in Charge Shawn Martin and Willie Johnson. Willie Johnson was the Special Agent in charge of Special Agent Lucinda Beverly. He would have been the one to authorize her investigation into GOD and for that he was on her list as well.

Intel showed Special Agent Beverly left every day at 5pm regardless of what was going on. Dominique and Desmond watched as Beverly left the building and was stopped by two guys that looked like they were agents as well from the way they dressed to their stature. *"That must be Agent Patrick and Agent Pennington."* Dominique thought.

She had been told this trio were the ones that had somehow infiltrated GOD's organization. Agent Beverly chopped it up with her crew for a couple of minutes and then she hopped into a money green Nissan Pathfinder and started her vehicle up, but she didn't pull out. It wasn't until a white Avalanche pulled up next to the Pathfinder that the agents began to pull out of the parking lot with the other vehicle in tow.

They made a left at the light onto Military Highway with Dominique at least three car lengths back; she looked over to Desmond and attempted to answer some of the questions that were sitting in the worry lines that ran across his forehead.

"Those are the FBI assholes that got the evidence to lock up my pops, I want to find out how they got it... and then cancel their ticket."

Dominique knew Desmond was a Navy Seal but that didn't mean he was made for this street shit, and killing FBI agents might not be on his play list. He better man up or he would get it too if that's what it came to. Dominique looked over at him when she stopped at a red light. She could still see her prey ahead and they were now in the right hand turning lane close to the 264w exit.

"Looks like we are headed to the interstate," Dominique voiced just to make conversation.

Desmond was hard to read and Dominique really wasn't one for beating around the bush so she was just going to ask him.

"So Desmond, are you good with what I have to do or do you want me to drop you off?"

Even though she felt he was hard to read his face was an open book now. The look he carried was a cross between anger and disgust

"What you think I can't handle myself or I'm going to fuck up your Op?"

That took Dominique by surprise and not much did. For some reason she wanted to reassure him and she couldn't put her finger on the reason but went with it anyway by saying,

"That's not it, I'm sure you can but I don't want to draw you into something you don't want to get involved in." This olive branch was extended with so much care it even surprised her.

That seemed to calm Desmond because the look in his face returned.

"I am apart of GOD's army just like everybody else, so don't get it fucked up Dominique. now drive."

Dominique smiled deep inside cause she knew she had a rider on her team. She followed her prey as they turned right and hopped on 264 headed towards Virginia Beach. The drive was silent but the thoughts that ran through Dominique's mind were wondering where these guys were going and focus on executing the rest of her plan. Taking the Independence Blvd exit Dominique followed the unsuspecting crew to Holland Rd and Lynnhaven Blvd. When the group pulled into the shopping center on the right and parked in front of Barry's Lounge Dominique passed them up and made a U-turn. As she passed them something caught her eye. She started to let it pass but the feeling she got at the pit of her stomach when something was fucked up was there. Desmond noticed the look on her face and said "What did you see, because I know you saw something?"

Dominique liked how on point he was but she wasn't sure she wanted to verbalize what she thought she saw. "Not sure yet, let me swing back around."

There wasn't a lot of traffic in this section of Lynnhaven so there wasn't much cover. Dominique was glad she drove the Lexus that could blend in with the other cars; she pulled into the shopping center and backed into a parking space away from the entrance.

"You see that dark blue Hummer over there sitting on 24's?" she asked Desmond. That's Shadow's Hummer. He has been tailing me for a couple of weeks, he doesn't think I know, but I do. I wonder what he is doing here and what he really has to do with what is going on."

Shadow sat at the bar in his hole in the wall spot. He was getting fucked up off of that Henn Dogg trying to figure out how he let Dominique give him the slip and wondering if his cover was really blown like his dad said it was. He thought to himself, *"Damn I need to figure out what my end game is here and if I want to continue to roll with Dollar ass. That nigga is going to have my mother buying a black dress."* Shadow saw the woman walk in flanked by two big ass motherfuckers. Just like every other man in there his dick immediately got uncomfortable in his jeans as he thought, *"Damn that bitch is fine as shit."* "Who the fuck is that?" he asked under his breath not thinking anybody heard him. The nosey waitress did hear him and smiled at him and came over and put him up on game.

"Shadow, I know she cute, but she deadly and she is also the Fed's so stay away from that bitch." The waitress whose name was Dina had been trying to fuck Shadow for years so she took this opportunity to put her ad in one more time. It wasn't unusual for Dina to be in the know, because her ass knew everybody. So Shadow was sure the sexy ass dime piece was indeed a Fed.

Shadow knew Dina wanted to give him some pussy. He also knew her head game was official since a couple of his boys had already sampled the shit, and looking at the way her ass sat out and her titties sat up almost gave Shadow second thoughts. But he didn't want the blow back up in his hangout spot. Because once he put the anaconda on her ass she was going to fall in love and he didn't have time for that shit.

Shadow told Dina she was like his little sister so stop trying to put that on him. The look in Dina's eye was not a look of a sibling but she let it go for now.

"Whatever Shadow, you better stop playing with me. "

Dina got her drinks and turned around to go serve her customers.

Shadow kept an eye on the goddess that walked in and put every bad bitch in the spot to shame. She had such a familiar look but at the same time he had never seen anything like it before. She kind of looked like a mix between Megan Goode and Halle Barry but that ass, shit that's all Beyoncé. Shadow was shook from his day dream by a tap on his shoulder.

"Damn, I'm slipping," he thought as he turned and was face to face with the goddess herself. He recovered quickly as he realized her slick ass was up to something.

"How can I help you agent uhmmm…"

Shadow could tell she was taken by surprise that Shadow knew who she was. She thought she was moving in silence and had planned to run game on Shadow and make him an unwilling participant of her team.

Agent Beverly decided to shoot straight from the hip, "I was wondering why you were outside of the Airport Hilton the other day?" Beverly had found out after they pulled out of the Hilton parking lot that Agent Patrick was able to get the license plate of the Hummer they saw in the parking lot and the records matched one Shannon "Shadow" Gibson, Jr.

Now Shadow was the one looking like a deer caught in the headlights. He couldn't believe she knew he was there, but it also made him wonder what she was doing there. Shadow decided to play it cool and not tell her shit so he lifted his left eyebrow and gave her a smart ass reply "Minding my fucking business and I would suggest you do the same."

With that he got up from his seat, put money on the bar and walked out of Barry's thinking, *"damn can't even chill in my spot without these muthafuckas blowing it up. They ain't even playing fair sending in sexy bitches like that, shit."*

Shadow was so engrossed in being pissed off he didn't see Agent Beverly behind him or Dominique watching from the comfort of her Lexus with a high tech directional mic pointed at the commotion. Desmond told her he was impressed by how well she prepared for her op. Dominique couldn't explain why her pussy was thumping but this nigga had that effect on her. She would have to explore that later.

Agent Beverly walked behind Shadow and put her arm on his shoulder to stop him from walking.

"Fuck you want you cop bitch?" shadow yelled.

The DP's who had followed Beverly out were about to whip Shadows ass but Beverly held her hand up to stop them. She looked Shadow in his eyes, Shadow had seen this look before and he knew it was the look of death. But what fucked him up was he had seen those eyes before and he had seen this look before. Her voice caught him by surprise because it was sweeter and more deadly than he would have imagined it to be as she said,

"Shadow please understand I will fuck your world up, your momma's world up, your punk ass daddy's world up, so you better not fuck with me because I am your worst nightmare…a real bitch operating under the cover of law."

Agent Beverly stepped back from Shadow and then put her finger in his face and said,

"When I ask you a question, or tell you to do something tell me what the fuck I want to know or do what the fuck I tell you to do simple as that."

By this time Shadow was surrounded by the DP's, but he didn't feel threatened. So he kept with his same aggressiveness in dealing with their ass straight letting them know, "Fed or no Fed I will fuck all three of y'all up. So if you ain't got no reason to hold me get the fuck out of my way or deal with my fucking attorney."

Special Agent Beverly reluctantly stepped aside only because she didn't have any legal reason to hold him. Shadow had called her bluff and she watched as he hopped into his Hummer and screeched out of the parking lot leaving her to contemplate how she wanted to use him to bring down the house GOD built. Agent Beverly knew that on paper he and his father were clean. Rolla owned a string of barber shops and Shadow was part owner in at least three of them. He paid his taxes; he didn't have as much as a parking ticket. But Beverly knew that's what the paperwork said, the streets were talking. And the talk was saying Shadow took after his pops as a cleaner for hire. The Feds were never able to make a charge against his pops but Shadow was about to make himself a target if he didn't play ball.

Dominique and Desmond sat back in the Lexus after witnessing the altercation between Shadow and Agent Beverly. Dominique had a new respect for Shadow because he surely wasn't buying what the Feds were selling. That told her two things; one is Shadow wasn't working for them and secondly she still didn't know why Shadow was following her. Dominique had a quick thought flash across her mind but thought to dismiss it. She knew when they were younger Shadow had a crush on her.

She started to think he was just on his lustful stalking routine but decided she better treat it as serious until she found out for sure. She made a mental note to hem Shadow up real soon, but right now she focused on Agent Beverly who was walking to her vehicle and the other Feds who were walking to theirs. Agent Beverly left first turning right on Lynnhaven and the other agents turned left.

Dominique took this opportunity to follow Agent Beverly to a neighborhood of townhomes off of Northwood Court. Dominique was ready to put the rest of her plan into action.

Two hours had passed since Beverly had entered her home. Dominique and Desmond spent this time getting to know each other. There was something about this man that intrigued her, normally she buried those feelings but sitting here with Desmond in this confined space smelling his Issey Miyake coming through his pours had Dominique's panties about to soak through her pants. He couldn't believe he was really sitting this close to Dominique. True he had been watching over her since the formation of the new Hit Squads but he normally did it from the perimeter. He knew what her reputation was; truthfully he really didn't believe the hype.

He thought to himself, *"This girl is just too fine to do all the shit I heard she does. I mean look at her neck, just thinking about sucking on her neck is making my soldier very difficult to control, not to mention those lips."*

The possibility of those lips holding his soldier hostage was making beads of sweat pop up on his head. This didn't go unnoticed by Dominique.

"Are you hot Desmond?"

There was no way he could allow this opportunity to test the waters go.

"You have that effect on me Dominique but I'll manage."

Upon hearing those words Dominique's heart began to beat so hard she thought she might need medical attention. She decided she needed to find a way to distract them from their current predicament so she started to discuss what her plan was for Agent Beverly because she had yet to share it with him. Dominique always worked alone on projects unless she was working with Jamal or Monique. She nervously cleared her throat and stared out the window as she began to speak.

"This Bitch somehow came across the evidence to lock my pops up, but the evidence she got could only come from someone close to my operation."

She turned to look Desmond in his almond shaped eyes that appeared to turn from a shade of green to a goldish brown and swallowed hard and tried to continue without showing him how much he was affecting her. "I plan to snatch her up and watch the other two to see where they lead me."

Dominique looked deep into Desmond's eyes to see if she could spot any bitch in him. She needed to know now before shit popped off, but real recognizes real and he was a true soldier. So she continued with her thought, "I like that plan because they are bound to flip when she is off the scene, she is obviously the brains."

Just then the lone light that had been illuminated in the townhouse finally went out.

"Let's give it another thirty minutes and then we will go in." Dominique said as she began checking her hit bag for duct tape, rope, and chloroform finding all she needed in place. Desmond was silently impressed, but he would reserve his final thoughts until he watched her in action. He knew he made Dominique nervous, he could tell by the way she diverted the conversation back to all business. He didn't plan on sitting in the car and talking business for the next thirty minutes. He wanted to know if he had a shot or if he should just stick to business, but he knew he couldn't act thirsty with Dominique. She was used to men falling all over her.

Desmond had watched Jamal be at her beck and call when it was obvious to Desmond he was not her man so he decided to take a different approach.

"I hope this runs smoothly because I haven't been home in a week and my lady is beginning to think I am out cheating."

He got his answer by the recoil he saw in Dominique's body language. She probably wasn't even aware she did it because he was sure she would never let him know that she was feeling him. But that knowledge alone was enough for him to hope she would come to him one day soon.

Dominique was not surprised some woman had a firm grip on Desmond because if he was her man so would she. She was more disappointed that he wasn't available, or was he? Did mystery woman have his heart? Dominique decided she was going to find out. It had been a while since she was interested in anyone and she wasn't willing to let that attraction go that easily.

Thirty minutes later they were at the back of the townhouse while Desmond watched Dominique quickly dismantle the home security system and pop the back door lock with precision skill. She led them through the house as if she had been there before. What Desmond didn't know was she had been in the home several times and had placed listening devices and video surveillance throughout the home. Dominique attacked the stairs like a panther, determined but stealth. She was so low to the ground you would of thought she was about to crawl, but the quickness in her actions was what caught Desmond's eye. Once they reached the top of the stairs they could hear the faint sound of music coming from the room to the right. Dominique knew this to be the master bedroom from her surveillance so she moved slowly towards the room keeping her back pinned to the wall with Desmond closely behind her.

The music was louder as they got closer to the room and she noticed it was Prince's When Doves Cry and she uncharacteristically thought to herself she loved her some Prince. They were outside of the room and it was time to make a move so Dominique slowly pushed the door open silently glad it didn't make any sound. Agent Beverly appeared to be sleeping and unaware she had two deadly killers in her room but as the killers approached the bed Desmond immediately knew something was wrong by the look of the lumps in the bed. He grabbed Dominique by her shoulder and threw her down on the mattress just as a silenced shot went over their head. Dominique and Desmond didn't have time to think, their instinct and ability took over and they rolled off the bed and headed in the direction of the shot in opposite directions.

Agent Beverly realizing she had unprepared to go all out on her next attack. She had already made a call to the DP's and if she could just hold out until they arrived she would be good, but since there were two of them she decided to lay in wait and blast anything moving.

Dominique knew she was dealing with a trained killer, she also knew there is a distinct possibility she had already called for backup. What she didn't know was how Agent Beverly knew they were in the home. I'll just have to ask her, she thought. Dominique made eye contact with Desmond to create a diversion. She watched as he made animalistic stealth moves toward the walk in closet door.

He looked so sexy in his movements she momentarily forgot why she was there; all she could think about doing was ripping his clothes off and fucking his brains out.

Dominique knew she was going to have to find out why she kept getting side tracked around this man she hardly knew. The sound of gunfire coming from the closet brought her back to the mission at hand and while Desmond had the gun trained in his direction Dominique came from the opposite direction and shot Agent Beverly in her arm causing her to drop her Glock and drop to her knees. Before she made it fully to the ground Desmond had her wrapped in a bear hug and Dominique was tying her hands behind her back. The killers made quick use of the duct tape and quickly made their way down the stairs and into the back yard.

Dominique was secretly glad to have Desmond with her because he just threw the injured agent over his shoulder like she was a pillow. They dropped her into the back seat of the Lex laying her down so it didn't look as though there was a back seat passenger. As they made their escape from the neighborhood they could hear the sirens in the distance. But it was too late. They were like crack heads on this caper and you know you are not catching no crack heads. With their great escape they never saw the black Dodge Magnum SE following close behind.

TONYA GREEN

There was never any question in her mind if she was going to take over GOD's case and rescue him from the jail that held him. Tonya Green had been waiting to rescue GOD long before the law came into the picture. She could still remember the first time she saw him in person like it was yesterday.

He dropped the twins off at the dorms on the campus of Hampton University to get settled in. When he walked in the room Tonya's breath literally left her body; she could not remember that ever happening before. The chiseled features of the magnificent creature before her had her normally reserved behavior betraying her and before she knew it her body took over her mind and she was approaching the man of her dreams.

"Excuse me and welcome to Fisher Dorm." She hoped she didn't sound as scared as she felt at that moment.

GOD looked into the face of an angel and thought too bad she was young enough to be one of his daughters. So he played it cool like he really wasn't having a hard time keeping his eyes off of her; she was absolutely beautiful. Her skin was the color of melted butter and eyes were way too serious for a woman so young, but the look of determination is what caught his attention. No one had ever had this effect on him since his Jewel was with him; that's when he knew he was in trouble. GOD had never been so glad to hear his oldest calling his name and he knew right then he would limit his visits to Fisher Dorm.

The memory was so fresh. Attorney Green sat in the hollow and musty smelling room reserved for attorneys to meet with their clients anticipating seeing GOD again. It had been at least five years since she last laid eyes on him. *It was at her graduation, she was a third year law student when GOD dropped his twins off at Hampton.*

She was surprised to see him in the audience at her graduation; she spotted him before he saw her. She remembered wondering who he was there to see, instantly getting jealous. Imagine her surprise when he walked up to her after commencement and hugged her from behind. GOD told her not to talk, he gave her the most luscious kiss she ever had and told her that if she still felt the same way in five years to come find him. GOD then handed her a beautiful Tiffany box and disappeared.

Tonya had her associates working on his case and was using "special circumstances" to gain deeper insight into the fight ahead. She could hear the boots of the corrections officer coming down the corridor and the anticipation of seeing GOD again was making her perspire. Her normal cool demeanor was effected and Tonya did not like it one bit. She knew he had this effect on her, that is why she stayed away, but after getting the call he wanted to see her, she had to. How do the young folks say it, she thought, oh yeah man-up. So here she sat and before she could think on it anymore the door opened and there he stood still as handsome as she remembered. Still all man, still the man, and her body and mind still reacted the same way. "*Damn*" was all she could say to herself.

GOD decided to save her, because he knew the effect he had on her. But what she didn't know, couldn't know, was she had the same effect on him.

"Hello Ms. Green I appreciate you taking time out of your busy schedule and coming to see me yourself."

If she didn't know any better Tonya would have sworn she heard a hint of sarcasm in his voice. But why would he care who met with him, as long as we were working overtime to get him out of here. Tonya's mind was working overtime but she couldn't focus on that right now.

"Mr. Dunbar I assure you my associates are working to get you out of here and back to your family."

The corrections officer closed the door and his boots could now be heard fading away as he made his way back to his post. Tonya decided not to waste any time in bringing him up to date with where they were in the case. She decided against giving him the gory details, thinking,

"I don't know why I don't tell him what I'm doing; he goes hard and deserves to know. I just don't think I am ready to share that part of my life with anyone, definitely not GOD. I don't want him to think differently about me. So I will just keep this to myself."

Tonya put on her best attorney demeanor which put you in the mind of that chick Alexandra Cabot, the assistant district attorney on the TV show Law and Order. Tonya loved that show.

"Mr. Dunbar I believe we are making some progress in your case. There appears to be some question about the tactics of the Feds in obtaining the evidence against you; my associates are working on that aspect of the case. We are also attempting through discovery to get access to the government's confidential informant. It appears your original attorney Marcel Hawkins did not even request this initially. But it turns out he may have had a drug problem that may have hindered his ability to be effective on your behalf. These matters have been brought to the judge's attention through the form of a motion and we are awaiting a call from his clerk as I speak."

Tonya was speaking so fast she never noticed GOD appeared to be looking through her. She never noticed there appeared to be something else on his mind. Her original thought was what could be more important than the possibility to get out of this hell hole, and then it hit her, something must be wrong with the twins.

"Are the twins ok?"

The intensity in GOD made Tonya weak

"What is it GOD?"

She never called him that. He didn't even know if he wanted her to call him that. Being here with her like this, even like this was working havoc on his reserve. Her scent was tickling his nose and making his man stand at attention. He tried to place the scent but it was taking too much energy.

Fanita Moon Pendleton

"Look Tonya some shit is about to go down and I feel like the twins may be in danger. I need you to get me the fuck up out of here, there just ain't no other way to say it, do you understand me baby?"

GOD's demeanor was as regal as ever and the deep baritone in his voice would melt any woman's heart, but there was an undercut of seriousness she couldn't ignore. Tonya was as close as a sister to the twins, who she took under her wings when he dropped them off at college. She stayed involved with them even after she graduated. GOD always loved her for that and in the back of his mind and heart he always knew eventually he would bring this woman into his life. Tonya felt even more compelled to get him out. GOD looked at her again and said, "Here's what I want you to do, I need you to find grounds to get me before the bench to have a new bond hearing. I have no previous criminal history and I am a gainfully employed business owner with Dunbar Realty. There really is not a good reason you should not be able to secure my release."

There was a look of surprise on Tonya's face but at the same time she felt this man who made her lose her professional self from just thinking about him could do anything.

"Don't look at me like that Tonya. I graduated from William and Mary Law. I just never took the bar."

GOD could tell he had succeeded in unraveling the rest of the beautiful Tonya Green's demeanor. She had that who is this masked man look in her eyes.

He relished it because he had seen a similar look all those years ago when he first started courting Jewel. GOD felt a burning sensation. It was near the part of his heart he kept locked for over twenty years.

Tonya could feel something happening as well and knew it had nothing to do with the law. She wanted to save face so she quickly gathered herself and said,

"I will get right on that Mr. Dunbar and get word to you through one of my associates as soon as possible with the progress."

She gathered her notes and placed them back into her Coach briefcase. She tried her best to remain calm as she pressed the buzzer to alert the guards she was ready to go. She stood facing the door almost opening the door with her mind. Tonya didn't hear the sound of boots yet, but she did feel GOD's breath on her neck as he trailed small intimate kisses from her ear down the nape of her neck. Tonya could hear somewhere in the distance space in her mind Aretha Franklins "Dr. Feel Good" and despite herself Tonya let out a loud moan. She closed her eyes and pretended this was her husband making her feel this way. God pressed his 6'5 frame up against her and whispered so softly in her ear it instantly caused her juices to flow down her leg.

"Something is always happening between us….we just both continue to fight it…. But we are not strong enough to win; this time…..do you want to keep fighting baby? Do you want to let me in baby?"

As he was whispering in her ear GOD took his hand and lifted Tonya's skirt and slipped his fingers into the juiciest pussy he had ever felt. "Damn T, this is mine, you understand me?"

As he said those words to her he stroked her pussy and teased her clit to the point of no return and before you knew it there were two sounds that were distinctive, the guard's boots getting closer and Tonya yelling at the top of her lungs from the orgasm she just had.

"URRRRGGGGG Oh my God URRRRGGGG I LOVE YOU!"

GOD attempted to muffle her cries with his tongue to no avail. The boots were louder which alerted them the guard was right outside of the door. GOD knew he heard Tonya because she was still whimpering and shaking which made GOD think to himself *"Damn this woman is sensual and I might have to make some changes in my life real soon."*

Tonya was embarrassed; she had done the unthinkable for a woman like her. She had given into the only man that ever tempted her in this way. She never let any man touch her the way she let GOD touch her, not physically but emotionally. She thought, *"What did he do to me?"* Tonya could not remember ever feeling the way he made her feel with any other man. She couldn't believe she told him her deepest darkest secret, she loved him. She pulled her skirt down, straightened herself as best possible and then she looked the man of her dreams in his eyes.

GOD held her close and then his juicy lips touched hers, his tongue danced in her mouth and then that same tongue licked her lips. Tonya took GOD by surprise when she sucked his bottom lip and licked his lips. Those two moves had his dick as hard as Chinese arithmetic. He pulled back because this was a problem that couldn't be solved right now. The guard knocked on the door making Tonya jump. God licked her ear and softly told her,

"Our time will come."

He kissed her eye and released her just as the guard opened the door. Tonya's professional demeanor took on a life of its own. You would never know she just had two fingers buried deep in her pussy.

"Mr. Dunbar we will be in contact soon."

And with that she walked out of the room.

FUCK

Agent Patrick sat in his office brooding over the fact he did not arrive in time to save Beverly from her intruders. It has been a week since he got the distress call from Agent Beverly. She was talking low and fast.

"Patrick...it's me...somebody is in my house....my motion sensors just went off but my alarm didn't... so it looks like they bypassed it... get here... come in soft but fast... I will hold them off as long as I can."

Patrick remembered before he could ask any questions the phone line went dead. He knew she could handle herself; he knew she was built for this shit, but he couldn't stop the feeling he had deep in his heart.

Agent Pennington was at the other desk in the office lost in his thoughts as well. The look on his face matched Agent Patrick's. He recalled looking at a confused Pennington when he hung up with Beverly with a look on his face as if he was sensing something was wrong.

"Penn we got to get to Bev... someone has bypassed her alarm system and they are in the house... I know she can handle shit... but I got a feeling about this."

Pennington was driving and didn't hesitate to whip the white police issued Avalanche around and point it in the direction of Beverly's townhouse while cussing out loud.

"Fuckkkkk! I knew we should have followed her home, shit is getting real out here and we are bound to be targets. These muthafuckas do not want it with us. They can't fuck with the type of gangsta that we are equipped with."

It wasn't that Patrick wasn't feeling what his partner was saying, he knew as well as anyone the type of pain they could inflict, but he was worried about Beverly and couldn't shake the feeling shit was about to get out of their control. Patrick stared straight out the window with death in his eyes.

"I hear you Penn, cause if anything happens to her this city is going to burn, word life, it's going to fucking burn,"

The Avalanche made the right into agent Beverly's neighborhood with their vehicle lights out and parked five townhouses away. The neighborhood was quiet and no one was outside. Several houses had minivans parked in their driveways and most home's porch lights were on. They exited the vehicle and made eye contact, both of their eyes held the promise of pain to whomever they found in this house. Neither of them wanted to acknowledge what was behind that promise, instead they made their way to the townhouse deciding to enter through the backdoor.

They immediately knew what they would find wasn't going to be good because the back door was wide open. They both stared at each other the fear apparent in both of their eyes. Patrick broke the silence with a strong whisper,

"Fuck!"

They entered the home and secured the downstairs before making their way to the stairs and climbed the stairs with the swiftness of a poisonous snake on the attack. Patrick made his way swiftly to Beverly's room followed intently by Pennington. They listened for any sound of intruders or life but all they could hear was an old-school R&B cut by Otis Redding playing on the radio. The tension outside the door was thick but the DP's had been in thick situations before. From a crouched position Patrick pushed the door open and Pennington was close on his heels. They scanned the perimeter of the room and not seeing Agent Beverly, Patrick begin to show signs of worry. He moved towards the light in the closet and Pennington approached the door quickly. The music in the room seemed to slow down and the DP's felt like they were moving in slow motion even though their movements were far from slow; their movements were calculated and deadly. Patrick opened the door with his breath held not sure what he was going find. To their surprise and disappointment the closet was empty except for a trail of blood that led from the closet and pooled on the carpet. They shared a look of fear and anxiety as they began to search the home. After an exhaustive search the house was found to be empty; they were too late, she was gone. Pennington was the first to break the silence knowing they had no time to waste.

"If they wanted her dead, she would be right here, so let's get her back." He tried to make his body language convey the confidence his voice was attempting to put out.

Shoot First Ask Questions Never

Patrick knew Pennington was right, he just couldn't shake this feeling that he had... it took a real skillful person to get the drop on Beverly.

"Tell you what; whoever did this knew what they were doing because Beverly is the best at what she does."

As Patrick turned to leave the closet he noticed something shinny sticking out of one of Beverly's coat pockets, it looked like some pink notebook paper, but he couldn't be sure so he reached for it. It was a note and the writing looked as if a child had written it and it was written with what looks like a makeup pencil.

"Check this out Penn; it's a note from Beverly. It says there are two of them a man and a woman, smart and deadly."

Pennington jolted Patrick back to reality when he slammed a hole puncher sitting on the desk onto the floor. He scratched his head as he looked at the note that Patrick was still focusing on a week later. They both concluded the only man and woman team that has this level of skills and this level of balls is Dominique and Jamal. Both agents believed Dominique was dangerous and bold enough to make this type of move. The thought of this level of violation had Patrick's blood about to boil. The agents had a BOLO (be on the lookout) out for them for a week and had come up empty. Neither had shown up at their normal spots. The agents had some new leads they planned on checking out today.

They had to first get past Special Agent in Charge Willie Johnson, who was beyond pissed with the situation and felt something was not right about his agent being missing. He had called in reinforcements from the DC field office and he was pissed at Agents Patrick and Pennington. They both made an effort to stay out of his way because they had their own plans for whoever had Beverly.

STASH HOUSE

Monique was in the process of putting her plan into action. The drought would continue until muthafuckas started flushing out who the snitch was. But that was the least of her problems; Uncle Dollar has been trying to see them on some real gangsta shit. All of the stash houses had been relocated just as she instructed.

The main stash house contained the bulk of money collected from all of the other spots ran by GOD's army. The house also doubled as Dominique and Jamal's office. Once all of the money was dropped off Dominique had it counted and packaged. Some of the money was funneled into their legitimate businesses where payroll for every member of GOD's army came from. Every soldier received a base salary, paid taxes, and had a pension. This was definitely one of the things that made working for GOD a long- term option. The men working for GOD were not your average street thugs and hustlers; they were all deadly and all hood, but they were the best and the brightest. Every member was either a college graduate or had served their time in the military where they developed a special skill set.

Monique recalled a recent incident when the main stash house was attacked

Three weeks after the meeting at the Airport Hilton, Dominique, Jamal, Monique and Marcus were at the main stash house. Monique was doing payroll, Dominique and Jamal were packaging money and Marcus reviewing security measures.

Marcus noticed the three men creeping near the beginning of the block. They were out of place for the neighborhood, dressed in all black with apparent masks pulled up on the tops of their heads. What the would-be assailants didn't know was the new security measures put into place included high tech video surveillance that covered the entire block. Marcus immediately went into attack mode, he popped open the gun safe while he called for everyone to come into the security room. After everyone was quickly briefed, they each took their predetermined stations. These stations were developed as one of the security measures to use in case of outside infiltration. There were also security measures in place for inside infiltration.

Monique was securely hidden in a corner in the main living area, Dominique took up the same position near the back of the building, and Marcus sat in the shadows at the top of the stairs so he could pick off from a higher position. Jamal held the position on top of the roof; he could easily pick them all off from here but was told to let them enter the home so they could get their asses busted wide open. Jamal was to catch any runners or any stragglers who were joining the party late.

GOD's army had their ear wicks in so they could talk to each other. Jamal alerted the team that three men, who appeared to be heavily armed, were approaching the house. Two of the men began to ascend the porch while the other made his way to the back. Jamal noticed they were not professionals; in fact he believed they were a little sloppy especially when they didn't attempt to enter the stash house undetected but instead shot the door with a sawed off shot gun and kicked it off the hinges. But they were not prepared for the gun fire that greeted them upon their entrance. Marcus popped quick holes in the first intruder's knees and he quickly fell to the ground in pain. The second intruder instantly returned fire in the area his friend was shot from as he rolled to his left into the main living area. As he swiftly moved from the floor to a crouching stance he tried to adjust his eyes to the darkness in the room, he could hear his friend whimpering in the entrance and he wondered where intruder number three was. Just as he was preparing to make an attempt on the stairwell he felt the unmistakable coolness of a Glock to the back of his head. He couldn't believe he had been caught slipping like this, he hoped it was his third partner in crime just playing a trick on him. His hopes were immediately crushed when the voice behind the Glock told him not to fucking move. That voice belonged to Monique.

Marcus descended the steps and dragged the first intruder into the main living area just as Dominique entered the room with the third intruder at gun point. Monique informed Jamal through the ear wick to stay on point. All three men were placed in the center of the room, they were looking around at each other wondering how they got in the position they were in. They knew whose stash house they were hitting and they were told to take all precautions. The intruders assumed if they went in hard and took the group by surprise they could kill them, all take the money, and make it to the strip club before the late show.

As they checked out the deadly twins both trained on them with Glocks they knew they had dreadfully underestimated them.

Dominique was the first to speak, as usual; she liked to get the party started. There was no question from her voice and her presence that despite her beauty she would fuck your world up. "I don't need three of you mother fuckers alive to answer the questions I need to have answered. So the first bitch ass nigga to say something stupid is going to get his wig split. Nod your mother fucking heads if you understand me."

The rest of her crew watched with their Glocks ready to spit fire as all three of the men nodded their heads up and down like bobble heads.

"Now somebody tell me who the fuck sent you dumb motherfuckers over here."

No one answered immediately; Monique took this as a sign of disrespect. Her twin was usually the one who would flip out, but Monique knew the streets were checking for how they handled this shit. Monique walked up to intruder number two. This bitch had the nerve to have a look in his eye like he wanted to do something; Monique put the Glock between his eyes and fired one shot. Blood and brain matter went everywhere. The other intruders were visibly shaken as they noticed the smile on all the other people in the rooms face. They finally began to understand just how serious this shit was.

Dominique normally liked to shoot first and ask questions never but decided she would ask the same question again and possibly after her sister's demonstration, she might even get an answer.

"Who the fuck sent you bitches over here?"

Intruder number three noticed he was the only one who was unhurt and determined that if he wanted to stay that way he better speak up now.

"We were hired to do this job by your Uncle Dollar."

Both twins shared a knowing glance; they had already come to the conclusion Dollar had some hand in this. But they wanted to be sure of how far he was going to carry this shit, so Dominique asked

"What was the job?"

This time intruder number one felt he needed to try and save what was left of his life. Although he was in pain from having holes in both of his knees he made sure to speak up.

"Dollar told us where to find this stash house. He told us Dominique is usually here along with millions in cash. He warned us she was deadly, but at the end of the day she is still a bitch. We were told to kill whoever was in the stash house and we could keep whatever we found."

Having received the answers they needed to hear Monique and Dominique unloaded into both intruders until their clips were empty. Marcus stood back and watched the two most important women in his life work. They were unlike any women he had ever known and he knew some women killers. With their anger extinguished for the moment, the twins called Jamal in and the four of them began to plot their retaliation.

Dominique had been looking for Uncle Dollar ever since; but he had disappeared. He went underground when the bodies of his hired guns showed up on the door step of his Chesapeake home. Monique was now working on freezing the dope supply until somebody gave up Dollar's hiding spot. One thing is for certain, real ballers want to eat so she felt that it wouldn't be long before the streets started to talk.

Once she and her lil cousin Skillz met today she would be ready to move forward with her plan, Monique loved to work with her cousin. They jokingly call him the re-up man in the family, because he is the man that all outside crews see when they need more product. But they lovingly call him Skillz, because he definitely got skills moving the product. Skillz real name was Donavan Dunbar, Jr. He was the twin's Uncle Don's son. Uncle Don is Pops Dunbar's little brother and he always been like a granddaddy to both of the twins. Before they started calling him Skillz they simply called him DJ and he was more like a brother to the twins than a cousin. He stayed at their house all the time and he loved himself some Big Cuz, that's what he called GOD.

Their relationship was almost like father and son, GOD saw a lot of himself in Skillz and he always pushed him to do his best. Uncle Don was in the military so he stayed gone. GOD became Skillz defacto role model and GOD was determined not to let his Uncle Don down, so he looked out for Skillz.

I LOVE YOU

Monique could smell the Cool Water cologne before she even saw Marcus come into her study. The smile in her heart was because all she could think about was the last time he kissed her, the last time that he licked her. And if she was being honest with herself today all she could think about was how much she loved this man. He entered the study and walked over to Monique with a bounce that was so masculine and confident that she instantly felt her panties get moist. She knew the look on her face showed exactly what she was thinking. Marcus's deep baritone spoke up and shook her from the trance she was stuck in

"What you up to Mo, because you looking at me like you want to eat me up. "

"Now how did this man just read her mind like that?" Monique wondered if they were that connected thinking, *"Fuck it I'm just going to put it out there."*

"I just got to keep it real with you, that's exactly what I want to do to you Marcus."

Monique closed her eyes and licked her lips. She tried to stop herself from falling back into a lustful trance. When she opened her eyes Marcus was moving her ponytail to the side and licking the nape of her neck. Monique's mind was playing havoc on her senses as she let loose as she had never done before thinking, *"Why the hell did he do that shit?"*

Sensing her need Marcus put his tongue in my ear. The heat from his breath was making her legs weak; he literally had to hold her up. Marcus kissed her neck as he spoke to her in what she thought was the sexiest voice she had ever heard on a man.

"I love you Mo, with everything in me. I love you baby. I want to lick you so bad right now I'm tingling just thinking about exploring you inside and out has my nerves on ending. But baby I want all of you forever, and nothing less. So tell me when you ready to be mine baby, tell me when you are ready to carry my last name, you tell me."

Marcus gently took her hand and placed it on his dick. Monique's eyes almost popped out of her head. She had never felt anything so long and thick in her life. Monique knew she was a virgin, but she has seen his dick before. This was something different, he guided her hand up and down and she squeezed until she heard a guttural moan escape his throat.

"I love you too Marcus…..and I'm ready, baby. I'm ready." Monique knew the words she spoke were from her heart, she knew her father had given her the strength to make the decision. Marcus turned her towards him and licked her lips; this was so intimate, so delicate. He was always so gentle with her, but she wasn't having that today. Monique stuck her tongue down his throat and he picked her up as she wrapped her legs around his waist. He walked over to the sofa in the far corner of the study. Monique was crying, but couldn't figure out why.

Marcus was kissing her tears and whispering in her ears how much he loved her and would she please be his wife.

Monique didn't think she had ever been so happy in her life. She believed the crying was because she was scared to death, but she knew after the last talk with her daddy it was time for her to open her heart up fully to this man. Marcus sat down on the couch with her still in his lap, he laid her gently down and pulled up her Dolce skirt. Monique raised her ample and succulent hips to make it easier for him as he removed her thong. She marveled at how quickly her legs fell apart. It sounded like you could hear the wind. The smile coming from Marcus's eyes told her he liked what he saw but from his lips he said,

"I could look at you all day baby. I could taste you all day."

Marcus dipped between the most delicious looking thighs he had ever had the pleasure of kissing and he licked each thigh as he descended. The sound coming from Monique sounded like a new love song that hit a feverish pitch when he began to blow on her clit.

"Oh Marcussssss..."

"What baby, tell me what you want me to do, .I would do anything for you Mo."

Monique knew her eyes were rolling to the back of her head and about to pop out as he began to suck on her clit and hummed.

The vibrations that shot through Monique's body were the BOMB! Marcus cupped the cheeks of her ass and put his whole face deep in the pussy. Monique was dripping, more like leaking. She was silently scared she was going hurt her man.

"OMGGGGGG babyyyy you makingggg me... Oh... my... God... cummmmmmmmmm Oh my God!"

He would not let her go. She shook so violently you would have thought he was performing an exorcism. Marcus finally released her with a smile on his face.

"I love the way you taste baby. I want to open you up baby, but I don't want to hurt you Mo."

Monique looked into the face of the man that would give his life for her in a minute. No other man besides her daddy could have that distinction. She wanted him to be as deep in her as he could go.

"I want us to be one, I know it's going to hurt but I can't go another day without feeling you inside of me."

Monique sat up and licked his chest and told him she was ready. She took his manhood in her hand and laid back. She guided him to the special place meant just for him. Marcus's mind was on overload. He had wanted to be inside of her for so long his heart was about to leap out of his chest. He didn't think it was possible to love a woman as much as he loved Monique. Marcus took her breast in his mouth as he gently began to push his dick into the sweetest place on earth.

Monique thought it hurt like hell... but she was so safe in his arms the discomfort didn't last long before she began to feel so good that she thought she began to drool. The look on Marcus's face was worth a million bucks, his eyes were rolling in his head and he was moaning so loud in his deep baritone that although she didn't know what the fuck she was doing she knew her man was happy. Marcus didn't move right away as he allowed her body to adjust to his massive size. But he couldn't contain how good he felt, "Mo damn momma you feel so good baby, this is my pussy Mo, fuck yes, shit Mo damn!"

Marcus said all that to her as he slow grinded his 10-inch monster into her newly opened flesh. He kissed the tears from her face and licked her neck. Monique began to feel so good she decided to take it to another level. Marcus picked her up never disconnecting their bodies and sat down on the couch with Monique straddling his lap. She has never done this before, but she knew what it was hitting for at this point. Monique began to move up and down on her dick and take all of him like she was born to do it. Marcus put her breast in his mouth and sucked like a newborn baby.

"Ride your dick Mo, shit Mo ride your dick baby, shit damn momma. This is my pussy Mo you hear me baby?"

She wanted to answer him, but something was happening to her body and she couldn't form words out of her mouth. "Oh shit Marcus, what's happening to me? I feel..."

Monique began shaking and he just put his hands under her ass and kept pounding that monster into her until she went limp on his chest. Marcus was still moving deep inside of the woman who has changed his life while they stared each other deep in the eye. There was something there and they knew it was their bond for life. Just as Monique thought it couldn't get any better, Marcus moaned so loud he had to wake the nearest neighbor.

"Fuck! Shit Mo... damnnnn yes."

And he began to shake and hold on to her for dear life. Monique decided to go into overdrive and ride his dick harder and she could tell he loved every minute of it. They were breathing so heavy you would have thought they had both went a-round with Tyson. They shared a kiss so passionate it again brought tears to her eyes. Marcus made Monique a promise.

"I will always have your back baby, and I won't let ANYBODY hurt you, not even me." Monique knew she loved this man and she was tired of fighting it. He cradled her in his lap for the next hour as they basked in the glow of the love they were both ready to face head on.

He was going to be her husband. All of a sudden Marcus began laughing so loud and Monique couldn't think of what was so funny. She wondered what he was laughing at as she still sat in his lap dripping with sweat and smelling like the sweet sex.

"I forgot DJ is out there in the entertainment room waiting on you, that's why I came back here. I was supposed to be getting you for him."

"Oh shit. I know he is talking about our ass. Let me get up from here and go take a quick shower. Tell him I'm coming baby."

Marcus winked at her and said "I bet he already figured that out!" and walked out of the study laughing.

Monique couldn't help but smile deep inside. She was never one to shy away from a challenge or an obstacle but when it came to letting Marcus in she was scared. She smiled because now she felt complete.

"My man is official, just like my daddy and that's why I love him. Let me get my happy ass in the shower so Skillz and I can get this shit popping."

SKILLZ

Skillz was chilling in the sunken living room thinking Monique and Marcus asses just left him hanging. He already knew what their disappearance was all about and thought it was about damn time as he laughed his ass off. Skillz was not really one for wifen no chick because he felt they were too slick, but even he had to admit Monique and Marcus were made for each other. He believed Marcus was a real nigga, just like his Big Cuz would want for his daughter, and Monique is official. Not only was she down to earth, she was a go getta, smart as shit, deadly than a muthafucka...and super fine. A smile crept to his eyes as he thought if she wasn't my peoples, I would be trying to fuck, straight up. But both twins were like his big sisters, they were two years older than Skillz and he would straight up kill a nigga over they ass, niggas knew it too. But, with the training GOD put them through; they would murk anybody who crossed them before Skillz even got the chance to put his murder game down.

Smoking hydro and drinking up Monique's shit was how Skillz decided to spend his time waiting. His mind began to wonder how he could help get his cuz up out that muthafucking jail. The twins had business under control and he didn't doubt they could handle anything that came their way, but Skillz knew the twins needed his cousin's guidance and presence in their life. He knew the Dunbar clan was missing a part of the foundation that held it together.

It was obvious someone either in the family or close to the family was responsible for the bullshit and he wanted to be out there with Dominique shutting muthafuckas down. That was not to be because Big Cuz was adamant he didn't want him on that side of the business, even though GOD knew Skillz would pop his shit, he wanted Skillz handling the product. GOD believed his little cousin had a unique skill at leadership and organization so he was sure to put him to work where his talents would be most useful. Skillz did not questions GOD's judgment thinking it didn't matter which role he played he would always hold the Dunbar clan down.

About an hour later Skillz was fucked up and thinking Monique needed to get off that nigga dick and bring her pretty ass on in here. Hearing heavy footing coming down the marble floors he sighed, *"Oh shit here her ass come she must have felt me talking about her ass."*

"Bout time your lil ass got in here!" Skillz shouted before he looked up and saw Marcus coming around the corner grinning like a Cheshire cat.

"Fuck you grinning like you ate the damn canary for nigga?" Skillz yelled at his ass as he fell down laughing on the chocolate sectional.

"I ain't going even lie DJ, that's my baby and on my word niggas will get buried if shit get ill." Marcus had such a serious look on his face all of sudden. It just appeared. Gone was the sated grin he walked into the room with.

The look in Marcus's eyes let Skillz know Big Cuz had chosen well for Monique. Monique and Marcus think their being together was all on them, but GOD had always wanted it this way. GOD wanted a soldier of the highest caliber to hold his baby down and Marcus was that nigga. Skillz loved her too so he felt where he was coming from.

"I feel you cuz...that's my big sis... so I would be right there with you popping off on niggas."

Marcus had known DJ since he was in diapers so he knew what time it was with him. "I know that shit DJ...that's why you like a brother to me. Mo will be down in a minute, she say don't talk about her too bad."

Skillz was still laughing at their asses, but it was all love. Marcus fixed himself a drink and checked in with the other Hit Squads. The look on his face told Skillz some shit was popping off especially when Marcus turned to him and asked how long he was going to be out here with Monique. Once he was assured someone would stay with Monique he sighed holding a worried look on his face.

"Good looking out DJ let me go check on this nigga Desmond from Dom's Hit Squad. Some shit done popped off."

That shit really made Skillz laugh or maybe he was just high as hell because keeping it real, with Dom some shit was always popping off. Everyone knew Dominique's ass would set it off quick.

Marcus left to go holla at Mo and let her know he had to bounce and Skillz fixed himself another Henn Dog and sent a text to this freak he was putting the wood to and let her know he was going to be late; but to keep that shit wet for big daddy. Skillz laughed again to himself when he thought, *"Bitches love my ass. It got to be that Dunbar curse. We all some tall sexy muthafuckas... I don't know one of us who ain't over 6'4 and built for this shit, and if the rest of my folk holding dick like I am shit no wonder da bitches be all on us. Don't get me wrong I'm a suave nigga; patterned myself after Big Cuz so the hoes stay on me, but my dad Pop's D also gave a nigga some of that smooth Dunbar shit. I just got that shit coming and going and I keep them bitches coming and going."*

Skillz was only 19 years old and already had his B.S. degree in Marketing, his own mini mansion, a hefty savings both in and out of the United States and no kids. He did not have a steady woman because he kept telling the women he was not ready for all that. That didn't stop them from showing up. Right now Skillz only priority was family. Holding the Dunbar clan down and getting his big cuz back out here, simple as that. One way or another that shit was going to happen.

WHAT THE FUCK

Marcus went to let Mo know he had to bounce and DJ would stay with her. He still refused to call his ass Skillz. Marcus would always remember him as little DJ that used to follow them around everywhere when they were kids. He would always be DJ to him. Once Marcus got to Mo's room she was still in her Radius Blocks & Decora shower stall. He could see the outline of her perfect nipples, nipples that he had just been sucking on like a newborn baby. He felt his dick get brick hard just that quick, all he could think of was *"Damn I love this woman and as soon as GOD is home I'm going to wife her, simple as that. I want to plant my seed in her. I want to be everything she needs. I have wanted that since I was 6 years old."* The steam in the bathroom brought him back to his senses. Marcus opened the door to the large ass shower and couldn't take his eyes off of her raindrop ass, big and juicy just like he loved it. *"Damn Mo,"* he thought as he couldn't take his eyes off of her scrumptious ass.

She jumped a little, almost reaching for the automatic LCP Ruger pistol that was kept in the waterproof and fire resistant gun safe Marcus built into the shower. To many niggas have been caught slipping while taking a shower and Monique vowed she wouldn't be one of them. "Damn baby you scared the shit out of me, now you know I could have put some hot ones in ya ass, what's good?"

Marcus was laughing but he knew Mo would have lit his ass up, real talk. "I got to run and check on some shit that done popped off with Dom and her Hit Squad, DJ gonna stay here until I get back, that should give y'all time to go over y'all shit."

Mo knew some real shit must be up cause he never had to go check on one of the squads "Ok baby, be careful and Marcus?" The sweetness in Mo's voice made his dick jump right back at attention. "Yeah lil momma what's good?"

"Marcus, I love you with everything I have in me. I should have been told you that, but I was scared and you know I ain't scared of much." Monique walked over to him through the hot steamy water. You had to see it to really feel how sexy the shit was. Marcus's dick was begging him to stay but he knew he had to go. Mo took his face between her sweet manicured hands and she kissed him so passionately she once again confirmed why she was the one for him. Then she fucked him up, she begin licking his earlobe and she said,

"No one has ever been inside me before you and no one but you will ever put they dick up inside of me, because this is your pussy."

Now you know that just made a nigga smile like he won the motherfucking lottery. All Marcus could do was kiss her as deep and strong as he thought it would take to ensure her those words had stolen his heart. Marcus took her hand still dripping with water and he guided it to his swollen dick. She grabbed it through his pants making him quiver all down his fucking spine.

Marcus looked into her eyes and told her "This is your dick, another bitch can't even smell it."

They continued to kiss as the steam continued to fill the bathroom and probably would have still been there if Marcus's phone hadn't begun to vibrate breaking them from their trance. A quick look at the screen and Marcus saw it was Dom, now he knew this shit was serious because she never called his phone. It took everything for him to step out of Mo's arms but she already knew.

"Who is that Marcus?"

"It's Dom. Let me go check on this shit. I will see you in a bit."

"If she is calling you some real shit is jumping off, hit me on my cell when you find out what the deal cause if need be Skillz and I will right behind you."

Marcus held on to her for a little longer. His brain told him to go before he ended up on the floor of Mo's massive bathroom suite. He assured her he had Dom and whatever she had going on. Marcus made his way back through her bedroom and down the stairs. He let DJ know he was about to bounce and to hold it down and he was out the door. It was a nice night out so he decided to ride the BMW 3 Series convertible. Marcus never got to freak this ride because they always traveled in the big bodies; but tonight he was going to floss this even if he was flossing solo. As he stepped into the midnight blue with white on white interior all he could say was *Damn this bitch sick.*

When Marcus started it up he had to look to make sure it started, that's how quiet she was. He turned on the radio and it was like the radio knew what it was hitting for, blasting loud through the system was Dorrough's Ice Cream Paint Job.

Rolling like a big shot, Chevy tuned up like a NASCAR pit stop

Fresh paint job [Check]

Fresh inside [Check]

Is the outside frame in the trunk wide? [Yes]

Are the rims big? [What]

Do it ride good? [Good]

Lean back right hand on the pinewood.

Marcus pulled out of the circular driveway leading from the ten- car garage just as his favorite part screamed from the 14-speaker, 440-watt Bowers & Wilkins audio system.

Clean on the outside

Cream on the inside

Clean on the outside Ice,

Ice cream, ice cream paint job

Marcus normally didn't let loose like this. He wanted Mo for so long he couldn't really breathe like he wanted to until she was his.

Some niggas might think that shit ain't gangsta, but
Marcus would say fuck them, he ain't no gangsta.
Marcus was a soldier who just happened to be hood and
would put a nigga's dick in the dirt. But he was a man
before any of that and he loved the fuck out of Monique
Shakira Dunbar.

He bumped nothing but fire all the way to an out
of the way horse stable tucked back on land in the Pongo
section of Virginia Beach. Normally you wouldn't catch
niggas this far back in the sticks, but GOD owned all the
property in this section of Pongo and it was private
property, electric fenced, and fingerprint access only.
The only people who had access were GOD, the twins,
DJ, Michael and Marcus. They were also the only ones
who knew about this property. Jamal didn't even know
and he was high up in the organization so that tells you
how important the confidentiality and security of this
property was. Marcus pulled in front of the building and
he could see the lights were on and Dominique's black
Lexus was parked out front. He knew Dom was up to
something because she always was. He also knew it
must be something serious if she had Desmond with her
at the secret spot. Marcus was also surprised at
Desmond's ass. He put him on Dom because he thought
he could handle her. His military experience was more
recon and strategy than anything, but Special Op's is
Special Op's. Marcus wanted a thinker with Dom cause
she was both a thinker and a killer fo sho.

When he walked up to the entrance and placed his
thumb on the pad for entrance the thick bullet proof
doors announced his entrance although they had seen him
coming through video surveillance before he drove onto
the property. Even though this was a horse barn there
was not a likeness once you were inside. GOD wanted
this site to be multi-purpose. It housed living quarters,
interrogation quarters, and office space. There was also a
hidden basement that had an underground tunnel a mile
long that opened up to a shopping center where there
were two hidden vehicles for a quick escape. The back of
the building was older than the front building and not as
secure as the rest. Marcus was making plans to meet
with a contractor to ensure that section's security before
all the chaos began in the family. Upon entrance Marcus
heard music coming from the Interrogation room so he
headed straight there. When he stepped in he couldn't
believe what he saw. He expected to see Desmond and
Dominique even though he was hoping Desmond was not
here. Marcus heard coughing coming from the other side
of Desmond and immediately knew this was about to go
from sugar to shit.

"What the hell y'all got going on in here?"
Marcus asked as he made his presence known. They both
turned towards Marcus with different looks upon their
faces. Desmond was 6'6 and far from a punk, his
presence alone was intimidating. But he was a soldier at
heart and Marcus was in charge. Desmond held a look in
his eyes that said he knew he fucked up, but not
Dominique; the look in her eyes was one of supreme
confidence and accomplishment. She said

"Hey brother-in-law. "

She always said that to him because she knew how much he loved her sister and this was her way of saying she approved.

"Don't hey brother-in-law me Dom. Fuck you got going on here lil sis?" This is how she knew Marcus was not really mad at her. He knew Dominique was the truth and would not do anything sloppy or without thinking things through. She nodded her head towards Desmond and said, "Don't be too hard on Desmond, it was either join me or be left behind and I think he was smart to join me."

The wink she threw Desmond's way matched the look of amazement on Desmond face. Marcus could tell Desmond was gone. He done fucked up and fell for a Dunbar woman. Marcus could not be mad at him because he was a lost cause himself. Marcus was interrupted from what he was about to say to Dominique and Desmond by a continuous sound of sniffling. Marcus looked up and eyed them both for answers.

"Who is doing all that sniffling on the other side of Desmond?"

It was as if he asked the million dollar question. Desmond stepped to the side and Marcus could not believe who they had tied up.

"What the fuck she doing here? He yelled which was not his normal demeanor. Marcus could not believe what the fuck he was seeing.

JAMAL

You ever get the feeling some shit just ain't right? You really can't call it, can't put your finger on why you are feeling this way, you just are. Jamal had been having those feelings so he had been kind of laying low and chilling at his hideaway crib. He was trying to sort shit out and figure out how he was going to handle his family. Jamal hadn't really talked to Dom and for him that was different. He knew she was alright because the Hit Squad was watching over her, plus if he really needed to find her he could since he had a GPS chip put in her cell phone and Dom never went anywhere without her phone. Even though Jamal knew Dominique was safe something just didn't feel right. Dominique not trying to contact him just to check in made him feel uneasy or was that just his guilt?

Jamal's Hit Squad was on point. Marcus had hooked him up with some straight killas who knew their job. Dontrell was the senior squad member who ran the show. Dontrell did not look like a killer, he was 5'9 160lbs and coal black. He had been told his grey eyes were cat looking. His skills should not be underestimated because he was a martial arts master and an explosive specialist. Jamal liked Dontrell because he was easy to talk to and he didn't try to make pointless small talk.

Jamal walked in to the kitchen of his 4 bedroom condo and was once again in awe of how spacious and modern it was. Everything in his kitchen was custom.

There was the cherry Dynasty Cabinets by Omega, the champagne gold marble countertops really brought the elegance to the room, and all of the appliances were from the Kitchen Aid Architect III series. Most men would laugh at the way Jamal felt about his kitchen, but many didn't know he designed and installed the kitchen himself. Jamal fell into being a hit man by pure accident and just happened to be damn good at it. But if he wasn't killing and hustling he would have been an architect and a designer. He continued to reminisce about the life he was meant to have but could never fulfill as he walked into his sunken dining room and spotted Dontrell looking out the double-hung bay windows always on point. Dontrell heard him approach and turned slightly acknowledging Jamal with a head nod.

"What's up D, everything look cool?"

Dontrell continued to look things over before he turned to answer him, "Jamal everything appears clear, but you know how that is. I got all my men on post. Tyrell, Shawn and Aaron, so we good. What you got planned for today?"

"I'm going to try and catch up with Dom and see where she at and run by and check on some of the crew."

Before Jamal could say anything else they heard a loud crash in the living room. Dontrell was out of the kitchen in a flash carrying his silenced Glock 23 semiautomatic pistol. Jamal wasn't far behind with his trusted Sig Sauer.

When Jamal entered the room Dontrell was nowhere to be found but Shawn was lying at the base of the window with glass all around him and a bullet in the back of his head. Jamal immediately hugged the wall and got low, he knew some shit was coming his way. Jamal decided he was definitely not going out like Shawn; he was spraying whoever he saw moving. Jamal knew Dontrell was moving in the shadows and about to make muthafuckas have a bad day but Jamal was a nigga who made shit happen so he began to make his way through the living room and into the front of the house. He crouched down to get a better view of the room and who was lurking around. He was so engrossed in what he was doing he never knew what hit him when he was crept on from behind and knocked unconscious.

When Jamal finally came to, his hands and feet were duct tapped. The ceiling he was hanging from proved to be stronger than what he would have thought it to be. Jamal had a splitting headache that felt like it started from his toes. His eyes began to adjust to the light and he could smell the Cool Water cologne that resided in the air. He could hear light laughter and his mind began to wonder how he let himself be caught slipping. So many questions were swirling through the pain in his head like where was the Hit Squad? Had they all been killed? Jamal remembered the hole in the back of Shawn's head and figured they must have all met the same fate. Before he could think on it any longer a shadow appeared to his right and he was immediately slapped across the face with a gun. The slap was so powerful it caused his head to bounce back and Jamal could taste the blood curdling in his mouth.

Somewhere between the state of conscience and dreamland he heard it. A voice he knew too well and he didn't want to let his conscience mind believe it. Surely he still had to be in his dream-like state; but he knew it was true. He heard Dontrell speaking to him in a more aggravated tone than he had ever used with Jamal.

"It seems you have got yourself caught up in some shit Jamal, if you live or die today depends on you telling us what the fuck we want to hear."

Jamal decided to chance opening his left eye because the right one was completely damaged. In order to see who the "we" was Dontrell was referring to he strained to move his aching head to the right. He was shocked to see both Agents Patrick and Pennington. He was really fucked up; he searched his mind in an attempt to figure out what they were doing there and why they were kicking his ass. Jamal thought they had an understanding. He had done his part in supplying them the information needed to arrest GOD so he could stay out of prison. It was fucked up shit to do but Jamal felt his back was really up against a wall. He knew if Dominique ever found out what he did to her father she would not hesitate to put a bullet in his ass; or at least she would try. As fucked up as it sounded he knew he was truly in love with Dominique. But what the fuck was he supposed to do? The Feds had him cold on at least two murders. Quiet as he kept despite being the best cleaner on the East Coast Jamal was not built for prison.

Jamal really felt like fuck love because he was ready to get out of this life anyway. He had bigger dreams then this and ending up in prison was not part of his dreams. But look at his ass now, beat to shit and betrayed by the muthafuckas he was helping. Although he was barely audible, he had to know what the fuck was going on, so he lifted his head which felt like it had taken on a life of its own and now weighed in at 250lbs and looked at Agent Patrick.

"Fucks up Patrick? Why y'all busting me up like this?"

It really appeared Agent Patrick had fire coming from his head; his eyes had turned a dull shade of red. Jamal could tell something had really pissed him off but before he could answer Dontrell jumped in and said,

"Where the fuck is my sister?"

If Jamal wasn't confused before, now he was really fucked up. He didn't know who the fuck Dontrell's sister was and he sure didn't know why the Fed's were on him like this. No one looked like they wanted to hear shit he was about to say unless it was some real shit; but Jamal was at a loss. Agent Patrick was finally able to calm himself enough to speak and what he said next really fucked Jamal up.

"I am going to say this once and if I have to repeat myself I'm going blast a hole right through your dome. Somebody done snatched Agent Beverly. She was able to say it was a man and a woman before she was cut off.

Now the only people that come to my mind who would
benefit from fucking with Special Agent Beverly is you
and bitch ass Dominique. So I'm going to ask you once.
Where the fuck is Beverly?"

Agent Patrick bust Jamal upside his head again
with the gun just to ensure he knew this shit was real.
Jamal thought for a minute before he spoke mainly
because he had to get his mind under control from being
continuously bust upside the fucking head. He also
couldn't believe Dom would snatch Beverly. Scratch
that, yes he could believe it, but he couldn't believe she
would do it without discussing it with him. A man and a
woman, well Jamal knew it definitely was not him so
who the fuck was this nigga she was out doing dirt with?
Jamal questioned his inner demon as if there was an
answer on the horizon. Jamal surveyed the room and he
saw Agent Pennington in the corner with his eyes trained
on Jamal like a hunter to its prey. A deep sigh was
released from Jamal as he thought to himself Agent
Pennington never liked him and was once again wearing
a look as if he was ready to bust his gun. Jamal felt that
Dom had really fucked up; there were no two ways about
it.

It struck Jamal at that point Dontrell had called
Beverly his sister. Jamal bowed his head thinking, *"what
the fuck is going on?"* He turned to look at Dontrell who
was visibly pissed off. Jamal was beginning to see he
was going to die no matter what the fuck he said in this
room and he wanted some answers before they took him
out. He wanted to know what the fuck was going on

"D how the fuck you working for me and a federal agent is your sister? This was some inside job shit, y'all muthafuckas done set me up one too many times. What the fuck is going on?" Jamal yelled that shit as loud as his mouth and mind would allow him to. The look Dontrell gave him could melt butter. He starred straight through Jamal and he thought he wasn't going to respond.

"Jamal, you are not cut out for the dope game, for the crime game, or for the life. Your ass is not a gangsta. True you know how to bust your gun, yes you are sweet on your killing game, but you ain't got no heart. I always felt something wasn't quite right about your bitch ass but once these two told me you let my sister punk you into turning on GOD I knew then you was a bitch."

"Beverly is my half-sister. She doesn't fuck with me hard because she a Fed and I'm always on some grimy shit. But she my sister and I would fuck a nigga up for fucking with her. I don't give a fuck who it is. Nobody set your bitch ass up. Beverly didn't even know I was in the Hit Squad. But when the agents called me to tell me she was missing, it was a wrap, a wrap for you. Now where in the fuck is Dominique?" Dontrell asked with a menacing look that was sure to spell doom for Jamal.

Jamal knew life for him was about to end. The pain he was in wasn't just from his head, it was from the shit that Dontrell had just said and shit Jamal really didn't want to admit to himself.

TONYA GREEN

Attorney Tonya Green had been working on GOD's case personally since she left Northern Neck Regional Jail. She couldn't get the visit out of her mind. The weakness in her legs and tightness in her chest were still present even a week later. Tonya had never needed a man before in her life but she felt that she needed this man. Tonya was scared because she didn't even know if he felt the same way, or if he just wanted to make her work hard for him. Tonya began to think out loud, *"I am a very resourceful woman and I am an excellent attorney so I got some tricks up my sleeve."* What no one knew about Tonya Green is she had almost every high ranking city, state, and federal business man/woman and politician under her spell. Outside of handling her business in the court room she was also handling her business in the streets. Tonya was very discreet and that's why she was able to move in the shadows. She ran one of the most exclusive escort services in the state. The business was called Exclusive. The ladies were well educated, all having at least a Master's Degree; they were all what the young men call *all that and a bag of chips.* Let's just say they were every man's and in some case woman's wet dream. The ladies were not your typical run of the mill hoes or ladies of the night. A night with one of these ladies would cost you a minimum of $5000. They were companions for the evening able to accompany you to the opera or a state function.

They accompanied many of the city/state and federal decision makers. Celeste and Kindria were two of the most talented ladies and they were about to put in some overtime. Celeste was 25 years old, a graduate of William and Mary Law with a minor in business. She was 5'5, 130lbs with a body built like a goddess, and an exotic look which made it hard to determine her heritage. She said she was African American. Her mother was black and her father was Navaho Indian. Her hair came to the crease of her buttocks and was always styled to a T. Kindria had a PhD in biology; she was a mix between Puerto Rican and Italian which gave her the look of an Egyptian queen. Kindria stood 5'9 and moved with a grace most women would kill to have. Both women had careers but they choose to be down with Exclusive for their own personal reasons. They both had been working diligently on this special assignment.

Celeste was on her fourth date with the Federal Prosecutor Jonathan Williams. Williams had already proposed to Celeste twice. Judge Allen Roberts had scheduled a meeting with Kindria almost every day since she accidently bumped into him at a society function three weeks ago. Since the men both had a level of comfort with the ladies it wasn't hard for the ladies to catch them with their pants down; literally. They put the plan in place last week. The Regency Elite Presidential Suite had been previously wired for sound and video. Both girls escorted their dates to a political function and dinner and then retired to their separate suites. The plan was simple; get the men to let the ladies fuck them in the ass with a dildo and let it all play out on video.

The ladies thought this would be hard to do but they underestimated the hold they had on these very powerful men. What Tonya has found to be true in life is many of the world's most powerful men are pussies. They want to be dominated but if you ask them they will die before they admit it. Society dictates they run shit so that's what they do. But behind closed doors in many instances, they will let their hair down so to speak. Then they will let a woman, doesn't have to be their woman; take control. And that's just what the ladies did. When they put the sweet smile on and told each man how much more powerful the sex would be if they opened their mind and even took it a step further by performing anal fellatio. After that it was a wrap.

Both videos were something out of a porno. Both ladies had their conquest screaming and moaning like dick was going out of style. Tonya took the videos and had several of the graphic scenes made into print format with the ladies faces digitized off. She had an envelope hand delivered at 9am Monday morning to each man with a phone number attached.

The first call came in at 9:10am. Tonya knew it was Federal Prosecutor Jonathan Williams by the gruffness of his voice. But the usual calm demeanor he used was replaced with an anger that felt like an eruption. He cut right to the chase. "What the fuck do you want you muthafuckas?" Tonya let him get it out because she knew he needed to in order to listen closely to what was next.

She pressed the buttons on her Microvox voice changer to disguise her voice from a female to a male, *"let the games begin."* Tonya was pleasant sounding as if they were meeting for lunch.

"Federal Prosecutor Jonathan Williams, Let's make this short and sweet. You have something I want, and I have something you want."

"What the fuck do you want?" William's anger was reaching its boiling point.

"I want Lawrence Dunbar out of jail. I want all charges dismissed. I want it in 24 hours or the video goes to the news and print copies go to your wife, your employer, and your children's school. There is no negotiation."

Williams could be heard breathing heavy on the phone, gone was the bravado he initially had because he knew he was fucked. Tonya continued to give her ultimatum.

"There will be no further contact. How you get it done is your business, but I repeat you only have 24 hours to do it and there will be no extensions .Do you understand?"

Williams was so quiet at this point Tonya thought he had hung up the phone, but then she heard a piercing scream she was sure started in his toes. He was crying.

"Fuck out of here, wow I can't believe this shit, but what it tells me is that he knows shit was real...and would make it happen."

Finally his cry became a sniffle and he answered. "I will make sure it is done," with that she disconnected the call.

Judge Roberts didn't call right away; it took him 3 hours before he made the call. When the phone call came at 11am Tonya was immediately suspicious. She felt the judge did not take the threat seriously. Tonya answered the phone in the voice of a child thanks to her voice changer. The judge was immediately knocked off of whatever game plan he had originally set out to have. He calmly asked the child to put their parent on the phone. In her child like voice Tonya advised the judge her parent had written something down for her to read to him and she always followed instructions. Tonya then asked the judge would he let her read it to him. Tonya could feel the hesitance of the judge, so she pushed a little more by saying "If you don't let me read it I was told to hang up the phone and then those pictures would go out immediately." That's all it took as the judge quickly said, "go ahead sweetie and read it to me". Tonya read to the judge the same instructions relayed to Prosecutor Williams and told the judge she had to go. The judge tried to keep her on the phone and ask questions about her parents but Tonya wouldn't budge. Finally he got frustrated and hung up the phone. Tonya was satisfied GOD would be getting out of prison soon.

The deadline was approaching; Tonya decided she needed to get GOD prepared. She drove to the jail. She had not been there since her last encounter with GOD. Tonya was a little nervous.

She imagined her nerves were the same as a person who was sneaking drugs into the jail, her forehead was sweating and so were her underarms. It was the nervousness in her stomach that really let her know she was scared, but what was she scared of? What was this she was really feeling?

"Every time I think about the last time I was in these walls. I feel a certain level of excitement. Only one man has every made me feel this way, GOD."

DOLLAR

Dollar had to follow Dominique since Shadow's ass kept losing her. He already knew she was up to something since that damn attorney got blown to hell. He watched her and that big nigga carry the damn federal agent from her home and thought,

"That's your ass Mr. Postman, or should I say Mrs. Postman because one thing is for sure and two things for certain, Dominique don't fuck around."

Dollar hated to say it, but he knew his niece. He was not scared of her ass though and he was adamant she give up control of the business or lay the fuck down; simple as that. Dollar followed their ass all the way out to Pongo. He wondered what the fuck they were doing way out here in KKK country,

"Shit I don't have gas to be way the fuck out here and at a horse ranch of all places."

He decided just to sit for a while and see what he could see. Dollar was planning his next move thinking,

"All this cloak and dagger shit really ain't my style, something is going to have to give and soon."

When Marcus came up the road with his high beams shining and his music playing loud in his dark BMW 3 Series convertible Dollar knew it was his ole punk ass but he took his binoculars from under his seat so he could get a closer look.

Fanita Moon Pendleton

*"That is that nigga Marcus with his ole punk ass,
bet he still trying to fuck my lil niece but her tight ass
ain't coming off that pussy so he might as well try and
smash some other shit. What the fuck he doing? Damn
these binoculars get a nigga up close and personal. Oh
shit this nigga using his thumb to open the fucking door.
What the fuck they got going on out here? I got to get
inside this bitch fo sho."*

Dollar decided to call Shadow's ass and give him
directions to where the fuck he was at so he could have
some help with this shit. The other people he had
working for him were proving to be incompetent and
although Shadow didn't technically work for him Dollar
wanted him on his team. When Shadow picked up the
phone Dollar went ham on his ass.

"Fuck you at nigga? You supposed to be
following my niece. Fuck you quit on a nigga or what?"

Dollar could tell Shadow wasn't trying to hear shit, but
he didn't give a fuck. If Shadow was going to be on his
team he needed to learn who the boss was, simple as that.
Dollar realized he wasn't getting any feedback from
Shadow but not giving a fuck he pressed on.

"Look I picked up where you left off and I done
trailed her ass to a horse stable out in Pongo, put this
address in your GPS and come help a nigga out." Dollar
quickly relayed the address.

Dollar could hear Shadow breathing but he wasn't
saying shit. Dollar was unaware of the fury he caused in
Shadow until he decided to speak up.

"First off nigga, you keep getting me fucked up. I don't work for you and your shit is hot than a bitch cause a bitch ass federal agent and her goon squad hemmed me up outside of Barry's. Secondly nigga, I ain't fucking with GOD like that. This shit ain't no win for me so I'm out. Do you playboy but I'm done."

With that Shadow ended the call

Dollar didn't miss a beat. *"This nigga straight bitched up, fuck it I will do this shit myself.*

When I come out on top, niggas gonna wish they had fucked with me from the giddy."

Fanita Moon Pendleton

GOD

The days were becoming redundant. GOD spent most of his day reading; believe it or not he picked up a fetish for the urban gangsta novel. They way these authors told the story made him feel like he was still on the street watching shit go down. It kind of made GOD feel close to home. He would engross himself in that shit all day, niggas steered clear from him anyway which gave him the perfect opportunity to indulge without useless interruptions. Speaking of interruption, GOD heard his name begin broadcast like he won the fucking lottery or something. He jumped up thinking it might be one of the twins coming to share some good news with their old man. The deputies escorted him to a private visitation room. This immediately let him know either his real lawyer or one of his fake lawyers was there.

GOD knew who it was before he entered the room. She was wearing that scent again. The one that helped him sleep at night, the one he couldn't place but would be sure to keep her stocked in when he got out of here. He walked in the room and could immediately tell something was up, she looked different. She was still dressed to a T. She was wearing a bunch of Michael Kors, GOD recognized it because the twins always had him buying it, and she was wearing it well. But she held a look in her eyes, if he was not mistaken was a look of love. The way her chest heaved up and down had GOD transported to another place. Neither of them noticed the deputy leave.

Before she could say another word GOD had to know.

"Tonya tell me something."

Her eyebrow shifted as she looked him straight in his eye and said,

"Ask me anything you want to know Lawrence."

GOD kind of liked how his name came off of her lips, the juiciest lips he had seen in years.

"What's that fragrance you wear? I smell it in my dreams."

If he didn't know any better he would say Tonya was blushing. If you have never seen a black woman blush it's a beautiful sight.

"Well Lawrence it is called White Diamond by Elizabeth Taylor, do you like it?"

GOD closed the space between them in two steps and pulled her close to him. He ran his nose and then his tongue down her neck.

"I love it. "

Her breathing was heavy; she relaxed her head on his chest. GOD held her close.

"Tonya, I don't know when or if I am getting out of here but if I do, I want you in my life. I haven't wanted anything like that in a long time. Hell 21 years to be exact, but it's time, it's time baby."

When he didn't get an answer he tilted her chin up and kissed her eyes. Her tears tasted wonderful and he moved down to those juicy lips. GOD felt a moan erupt from deep inside. He knew he had to refocus so reluctantly he broke their embrace, but not before he expressed how he hoped to one day make sweet love to her. The look in her eyes made him want to say fuck it and lay her across the hard ass table, but she deserved better. GOD said a silent prayer he would be able to give it to her.

"So what brings you to see me Attorney Green?"

She let out a slight laugh at his attempt to bring order back into the room but what she said next made him want to heat shit up again.

"Lawrence hopefully I will have you out of here in the next 24 hours."

GOD was sure every expression passed through his face, excitement, happiness, caution, and elation.

"Please tell me how you plan on pulling this off baby."

Tonya went on to explain everything. When she first told him about Exclusive GOD couldn't believe she was the brain behind the money making venture. He had never used their services himself but he knew plenty of people who had.

Every person he personally knew had always given the ladies an A+ rating. GOD was surprised his little Ms. Innocent had so much business savvy and street sense. He knew right then that he had met the woman that would fit into his heart with Jewel and the twins.

"Ok Tonya so let me get this straight, do you think this will work?"

"I tell you what baby; if I don't work then you will see a scandal to top all scandals at city hall. But I know these men; they cannot afford to have this scandal. Williams is trying to be a judge and Roberts has aspirations to move into the White House, they will want this to go away." By the time she was finished with the news GOD could actually envision a future, a future out of jail, a future out of the game (retired but available to the family for consultation); a future with her.

"Wow baby I don't know what to say. I'm glad you are coming through for me like this."

Tonya had almost a childlike look on her face but when she opened her mouth to speak it was pure sex kitten and GOD felt his soldier growing on his leg.

"I think I have been in love with you from the first time I saw you, but I knew you would only see me as a little girl. I was hoping and praying one day you would see me as a woman, your woman and give us a chance."

GOD recalled the first time he saw her when dropping the twins off, and yes he could tell that she was infatuated with him. She was right, he looked at her like a little girl who was not ready for the big league, but every time he saw her she left a little bit of herself with him. In the way she carried herself like a lady, her career choices, her sophistication, her personality, and that round ass didn't hurt the situation at all. GOD sat back in his seat and looked into those intense eyes and told her he was ready. Before she could say anymore the deputy burst through the door and told GOD the warden wanted to see him right now.

MONIQUE/SKILLZ

Monique and Skillz were supposed to be talking business but Skillz was full of jokes talking shit about her and Marcus finally fucking. Monique told him he thought his ass was a comedian like Kat Williams up in here. She had to bring him back to earth because he and the Henn Dog were feeling it for real.

"Skillz are you in any shape to talk business because we can do this in the morning?"

It was as if she had slapped him across his face. He was sober real quick.

"Come on sis, you know damn well I am all about business. I was just fucking with you, lets rap."

Before Monique could even go any further her two way chirped and she heard the sexy sound of her man's voice but there was an undertone of pissed off that could be heard.

"Mo I need you and DJ to come to the stables, NOW."

The sound in Marcus's voice was different than Monique had ever heard coming from him. Gone was the easy going and sexy baritone. Monique knew something was clearly wrong and she didn't question him.

"We are on our way."

Skillz knew something was up too and was already up and ready to roll. He made sure he was strapped and turned to Monique and said "Let's get it cuzzo."

END IT

Jamal knew his life was over; he also knew his life was cut short because of some shit Dominique pulled. His final fuck you was going to be to fuck up her world. He hung his head trying to think of a way out of his situation, thinking maybe if he gave her up they would let him live. Holding on to this hope he began to tell them about the GPS he placed in Dominique's phone. The men in the room jumped up immediately and surrounded him, but Pennington, who had not said much spoke up and said, "I always knew you were a bitch. Where the transmitter at?" At this point Jamal didn't care what they called him, just as long as they didn't kill him. He tilted his head to the ground but spoke up so he was heard.

"The transmitter is in my phone. If you pull up her name on my phone it will tell you the exact address where she is now."

Dontrell pulled the information up on the phone he had confiscated from Jamal earlier.

"BINGO" he shouted getting everyone's attention. Dontrell smirked looking at the phone quizzically "Fuck they doing in Pongo?"

Now that Pennington had an address and a lead he felt Jamal had outlived his usefulness. Pennington began to think to himself. *"There is no honor among thieves anymore. I mean the code is fucked. Who let weak ass wanna be gangstas like Jamal in the game?"*

Pennington who was heavy in the game before the military straightened him out all those years ago believed he would have never been fooled by Jamal's wanna be thug ass. Thinking about it was pissing him off even more. He walked closer to Jamal as the others were discussing the plan of attack and he raised his Desert Eagle and shot Jamal at point blank range. The sound was loud and reverberated off the walls causing the other men in the room to duck for cover. Before he left this world Jamal could see the determination in Pennington's eyes but he was more focused on trying to understand why the man hated him so much. He never noticed when Pennington raised the weapon.

Dontrell and Patrick looked up from their hiding spaces and saw a hole where Jamal's brain or lack thereof used to be. Patrick smiled because that is exactly what he had planned for the man but Dontrell thought it was reckless. He felt they might need Jamal for information if the Pongo information turned out to be wrong. Dontrell thought, *"That's where criminal thinking beats police thinking."*

Dontrell decided they needed to move on so he got everyone's attention as they planned their attack on the Pongo address.

PLAN OF ATTACK

Dollar decided to get closer to the spot and see where the weak points of entry were. He knew he would never make it in the normal way because of the fingerprint scan but Dollar had broken into enough places in his day to find the weak spot. The property was large in scale and very isolated. As Dollar made his way around the perimeter he noticed a part of the building looked as if it was older than the rest. It was connected to the rest of the building true but it wasn't secure like the rest of the building. There was no gate around it and upon closer inspection it did not require any special ops shit for entry. Dollar smiled inside because he knew he had found his entry point. Calling on his home burglary skills Dollar and the lock picker he always kept on his key chain, just in case, went to work on the lock. He was ready to get up in there and see what the hell was going on.

Dollar noticed the place was huge and he wondered if this is where they kept the product. Many years ago when Dollar still played a major role in the family business he always knew where the product was held, but after his pops got sick GOD put Skillz in charge of the product and Michael in charge of organizing the teams effectively pushing Dollar to a lackey position.

"What the fuck Skillz lil young ass know about running shit? I have always liked my little cuz but he think he is really running some shit. When I take this shit over either he is going to get down with how I want shit or I am going to cancel his ass too cuz or no cuz."

All the while Dollar was moving the file inside the lock as he felt the familiar pop and smiled to himself thinking. *"I still got it, ha-ha, now let's see what the fuck is going on up in this piece. "*

Dollar was about to enter the back door when he heard another car pulling up pumping smooth R&B. *"Now who the fuck is this?"* He decided to check and see who else was showing up to the party before he made his way inside the spot. He figured he better find out how many wigs he was going to have to split before he rolled up in the spot. Dollar retraced his steps back around the perimeter making sure he wasn't spotted and he was rewarded with answers rather quickly as he heard Skillz talking shit to Monique about fucking Marcus. Dollar didn't know why the scrawl came to his face or why he was pissed off but he felt himself saying to no one in particular.

"I can't believe she fucked that punk ass bitch."

If Dollar was honest with himself he would admit his dislike for Marcus came from his dislike for his father, Michael. Michael had effectively taken over his place in the family business. Michael and GOD think they are slick and no one knows. They think everyone believes Michael is just GODs best friend. But Dollar was far from stupid, which was the source of the fury boiling inside of him.

"So it wasn't enough to give handling of all of the drugs to Skillz but my seat at the table had been given away as well."

Dollar felt himself getting heated and willed himself to calm down so he could prepare to take back what he felt was rightfully his. Pulling himself together he decided he would deal with all of their asses once he was in the spot and situated. Still heated he smiled thinking *"I hope that pussy was good because that was your first and only taste."*

Dollar planned on saying this to Marcus before he put something hot in him. He returned to the back of the building and slipped inside unnoticed. Dollar noticed the large amount of boxes that were blocking his path and surmised this area was used as storage. Dollar made a mental note to comeback and go through every box. *"I know they got some good shit up in here and by default it all belongs to me now."* Dollar could hear raised voices and began moving in the direction of the noise.

Monique and Skillz entered the building and made their way towards the raised voices Monique quickly surmised where coming from interrogation room. She gave Skillz a smirk and they headed that way.

Skillz couldn't help but say it, "Cuz what the fuck Dominique up to now? Because you know this is her shit." He was laughing hard as shit and Monique had to join him because if anyone knew Dominique as well as she did, it was Skillz. and they both knew Dominique must be about to kill somebody. What Monique couldn't understand was why Marcus needed her there. Dominique done killed many people without Monique holding her hand so she wondered why now?

As they rounded the corner she could hear her sister talking shit to somebody. Monique and Skillz slipped in quietly to get a lay of the land as DOM went off again. Dominique's back was to the new occupants of the room. They went unnoticed by Marcus and Desmond as well. Monique couldn't see who had Dominique so heated. Dominique raised her left hand and slammed her 22 into the side of the person face and yelled

"You done fucked with the right one. I am going to ask your bitch ass one more time. Who the fuck supplied information on my fam and why the fuck you come after my Pops?"

The laughter caught everyone by surprise, it sounded as if it came deep from the persons gut.

"YOUR *POPS, YOUR POPS? MAN FUCK YOUR POPS! HIS BITCH ASS AIN'T SHIT BUT A DEADBEAT IN MY BOOK. SO FUCKING KILL ME OR I WILL SPEND MY DAYS MAKING SURE HIS NO GOOD, DEADBEAT ASS STAYS LOCKED THE FUCK AWAY! Y'ALL BITCHES THINK Y'ALL SO SMART! HAHAHAHAH JAMAL HAS BEEN WORKIN FOR ME THE WHOLE TIME. Y'ALL THINK Y'ALL SHIT IS TIGHT. BUT I AM THE SISTAH WITH ALL THE SMARTS! Y'ALL SHOULD HAVE NEVER THROWN ME AWAY. THAT'S WHY Y'ALL SHIT IS FUCKED UP NOW!"*

241
Fanita Moon Pendleton

Monique was listening to this crazy bitch, but she couldn't believe what she was saying. Desmond was trying to reach for a pissed off Dominique, but he wasn't fast enough and Dominique struck the bitch across her face so hard spit flew across the room. Monique could tell Dominique was hurt knowing Jamal was the one who was selling out the family. Better yet he was the one responsible for putting GOD away.

Monique was slowly creeping up while the captive woman was ranting. Marcus noticed her first and came to her side which alerted the others to Monique's presence. Dominique smiled at her and raised her hand again to give the captive, who Monique could now see was that FED Bitch, another knot on her head. Monique decided to slow Dominique up some so they could get some answers. She grabbed Dominique's hand on the down swing. Dominique was in a zone and she jumped almost ready to strike her twin before she turned and realized she was the one stopping her. She calmed down giving her twin and best friend in the whole world a chance to speak. "Dom if you beat the shit out of this bitch we won't get the answers we need because she will be dead, slow up and let me see why the fuck this bitch seem to hate Pops so much.. Something just is not right about that."

Monique knew Dominique had been on a killing spree and anyone involved in the case was sure to get fucked up. She also knew Dominique wouldn't rest until she knew who the leak was in the family. But Dominique's tactics were not going to get answers; they were just going to get revenge.

That's cool in certain situations, but right now. Monique wanted to know what the fuck was going on with this chick. She is harboring a huge hate. Monique wanted to know why the fuck she keeps calling her pops a deadbeat. Deadbeat must mean something else now days, because it can't mean not taking care of your kids or responsibilities the twins knew that was some bullshit. Monique moved closer to the woman duct tapped to the chair. Monique noticed she was very pretty. Even though she was seated she appeared to be about 5'6. Her skin was similar to the twins but she wasn't what one would consider a red bone. She still held smooth butter looking skin, but she was a shade or two darker than the twins Monique noticed. What couldn't be denied and Monique wasn't even sure if she was seeing things right. Monique rubbed her own eyes to ensure she was lucid. What she couldn't get over upon closer inspection was the diamond shaped eyes. Monique walked up so close to Agent Beverly she began to squirm in her seat. The intense look from the older Dunbar twin could burn a whole through you. It not only made you feel like you were on trial it made you feel like you were convicted and on death row, literally.

Monique could tell Agent Beverly didn't know how to take her. She didn't know what Monique would do. She was used to Dominique, but she didn't know underneath it all Monique was even more **DEADLY** than Dominique. The older twin let her younger sibling do her thang. The big guns were only pulled out when necessary. Something was telling Monique this would be one of those times.

RESCUE?

The drive to Pongo was longer than any of the men really wanted to endure. They talked all the way about their plan of attack. Dontrell felt as though the Agents were ok dudes. Not quite sure on which side of the coin they wanted to be, but he knew they honestly cared for his sister and would do anything to get her back and that was cool with him.

Dontrell began to reflect on his relationship with Beverly growing up and how close they were.

Beverly was more like a mom than his own mother. She cooked, cleaned, read to him and believe it or not would whip any body's ass on the street that fucked with him. Even though they had different dads, pops treated them the same. They had a good life. But there was a part of Bev that even Dontrell couldn't reach. He believed that's why she ran away and joined the military. They were never as close once she returned. Dontrell joined the service as well, just wanting to be like his big sister he guessed, but the constant separation and the choice of careers upon getting out of the service drew and imaginary wedge between them.

The car slowly pulled up to a huge property protected by an electric fence. Dontrell looked over at Patrick and Pennington and they both held the same questioning look on their face. It was Pennington who spoke what they were all thinking inside. *"What the fuck are they doing in a horse barn?"*

Upon further inspection the three highly skilled men noticed the security measures around the barn and immediately begin to strategize about points of entry. Patrick realized there wouldn't be an easy sneak attack but voiced his ideas. "Ok fellas we are going to have to make a statement here."

They watched as Patrick jumped out of the Lexus and opened the trunk, what he came out with next left all three former military men smiling from their feet to their eyes. It was a RPG-Rocket propelled grenade, most people call them bazookas. Dontrell knew right then he had underestimated the Agents. The original plan discussed had to be revised. Pennington suggested they blow through the entrance and rush the playing field. Dontrell noticed the bullet proof doors and pointed out the electric fence and video surveillance. These might be obstacles for average men, but not these special ops trained men with a single mission to save one of their own. They all reflected on Beverly's safety and began to plan a quiet extraction.

Agent Patrick assured he could bypass the video surveillance and fingerprint scan. Agent Pennington would handle the electric fence and Dontrell would handle the entry point. The men began to laugh because they knew GOD felt this location was secure. The remote location and security measures would change the mind of the average killer or thief, but the determined ex op's trained men would not be deterred. They were ready to bring all of their skills to bear to save the woman who has meant so much to each of them in different ways.

245

Fanita Moon Pendleton

They made preparations for the assault retrieving the AK47's and Glocks from the trunk and left the bazooka behind. Both Pennington and Patrick were putting on their ProMax Kevlar vest. Dontrell already had one on. He stayed ready so he would never have to get ready was his motto. He never went anywhere without his vest. All three men hit the ground and began to approach the building crawling to avoid the surveillance. Each moved fluidly as a unit as memories of years gone by came back. The look on their face showed they were in their element. As they got closer they split off in different directions. Patrick spotted the control box for the fingerprint scan and the video surveillance and removed his kit from his boot and began the process of dismantling it. Pennington found the rout wire for the electric fence and began to work on it and Dontrell analyzed the entrance for the best way to get in without being noticed. Entrance would be precision, but extraction would be deadly, believe it.

IM UP OUT DIS BITCH

GOD already knew what the warden wanted but he played it cool. If Tonya worked her shit as good as he believed she did he felt they were about to let him up out this bitch. As GOD entered Sheriff K's office he noticed how elegant it was. GOD thought about the man himself, K Harris was 6ft 5 with a solid build women describe as good looking. He is the youngest Sherriff every in Virginia Penal History at 45. Considered smart and personable and loved by his inmates and politicians a huge feat in any bureaucracy. GOD didn't admire many men, but he felt like Sheriff K was a man much like himself. GOD spied him sitting behind his large mahogany desk peering down into a file.

GOD cleared his throat and Sherriff K looked up and nodded at the open chair. The Deputy stayed by the door and was told to wait outside. He appeared to be apprehensive about leaving but one look from Sheriff K and he was out the door with the door with the quickness. He pushed his papers to the side and looked GOD in the eyes. GOD didn't know what he was expecting but hoped it wasn't fear. GOD liked the Sherriff, but would break his fucking jaw if he came at him sideways. Before he could finish his thoughts a smile spread across the Sheriff's face that reached his eyes. He began laughing so loud GOD almost joined him, but played it cool while Sherriff K said, "I don't know what the fuck you did, but these fat cats are scrambling to get you out of here. I mean that fine ass lawyer of yours has made some power moves, so you best believe your stay at my fine establishment is about to come to an end.

I am not sure when, but definitely very soon. You mind telling me how you guys managed to pull that shit off?"

GOD broke his gaze with the Sherriff, because he wasn't about to tell him shit, later for that. "Look Sherriff, I got a bomb ass attorney and I don't just mean her looks. I appreciate you letting me know what's going down." And with that GOD raised up from his seat effectively ending the meeting. Sherriff K didn't really expect an answer. He knew a power move when he saw one and he admired the man for being able to make moves. The Sheriff secretly wanted to be down with GOD's army and was hoping to use this meeting as an introduction. The Deputy entered the room and escorted GOD from the room with the Sheriff promising to send for him as soon as word came down about his release

BEVERLY

Even though she was tied the fuck up the fight in Agent Beverly would not let her give in to these spoiled bitches. Beverly felt like she was GOD's daughter too, so why the fuck did they get all the props, love, and affection? Beverly could not stop her head from spinning.

"Do I even want props, love and affection from my daddy? Wow, my daddy, damn I guess that's what he is, or could have been. But to me he is just a sperm donor who didn't give a fuck about me, so the hatred in me wouldn't allow me to feel anything for the daughters he chose to keep."

With this in mind Beverly looked Monique dead in her eyes with all of the venom she felt in her soul to answer the question she could see burning in her face.

"Fuck you and your GODLY image of your bitch ass daddy. Yo daddy ain't shit. He left my momma pregnant and penniless and never claimed me or attempted to lift a finger to help me, so fuck him and fuck you and your spoiled ass sister."

Before Beverly could get that last thought to rest Monique's hands were around her throat, she was pressing so hard Beverly knew within a moment's time her larynx would be crushed. Beverly could barely hear let alone see, but she felt pressure lifting off of her and voices began to come in clear.

She noticed Marcus and Skillz pulling Monique while Desmond held Dominique which he appeared to be struggling with. The men pulled the twins into another room. Dominique was yelling she was going to kill the Agent and calling her a lying bitch. Beverly could smell the rage coming from both twins. She knew the smell well. She wore it so much you could say it was her fragrance, RAGE.

TRUTH HURTS

Both twins were struggling hard and to no avail. Marcus was scared for Monique; she was so upset tears were flowing down her face. He knew she was at a place that would probably be hard to reach. A place he had never seen from her before but he knew where the dark place was. He knew if he didn't intervene Agent Beverly was dead. Desmond was having his own struggle with a screaming Dominique; she threatened to bring harm to him and everything he loved if he did not let her loose.

Monique was spiraling into a world she had never been to. A world where she questioned what she believed in. She had never known her father to lie to her or her sister. Who was this woman with her father's eyes who claimed to be his unclaimed child? Who was this woman, who has been nursing a hate for over twenty years? Monique being the most rational of the twins wanted answers. She was hurting and perplexed about what this meant in their life. She couldn't believe the man she loved and adored would ever abandon one of his children. GOD loved his children, they were his life, and this was Monique's truth.

Monique knew the private hell her twin was going through, because GOD and Dominique were her life and she would kill anything breathing that jeopardized the two most important people in her life. Monique wanted answers; she just had to get Dominique on the same page.

Everyone was so consumed with what they were doing they never noticed Dollar Bill in the shadows. He had been monitoring them since they came in the room. He silently wondered what the fuck had his nieces all to pieces. A part of him wanted to run out and comfort them, like he did when they were little girls. He did love them. Dollar knew whatever was going on with them was serious because these chicks never cry. He silently wondered if something happened to his brother. A part of him wanted to say fuck the take over and rejoin his family, support the girls in what they were trying to do. That was the part of him he refused to listen to. What he had to do now had nothing to do with love. The old phrase, this is business not personal came to mind.

"They got to go. GOD got to go. I am about to run all of this shit and they are in the way, simple as that. Family or not, I asked them to get down, and they wouldn't, so now they got to lie down."

Dollar stepped from the shadows and recklessly began to light the room up. The gun fire wasn't done with precision even though Dollar was an excellent marksman. His reluctance gave the others in the room the opportunity to prepare for battle. But not before Skillz skull exploded like a watermelon while a collective gasp went up in the room.

Dollar watched Skillz brain matter fly across the room as another bullet ricocheted off the wall and found its way into Desmond left shoulder. Dominique had enough; she took off in the direction of the mysterious shooter who claimed the life of her favorite cousin. She vowed with everything in her whoever this person would cease to exist momentarily. The smoke coming from her eyes and rising to her head was mimicked by the others in the room as they all focused their attention on the direction of the shots. All of the skilled killers made eye contact with each other and began to return fire and maneuver around the room causing a distraction for their attacker.

Dollar expected retaliation; he knew who he was dealing with. He also knew they better be ready for the fire he was about to put on their ass. From his concealed position he continued to coat the room with precision laid fire power, not sure if he hit his mark.

Dontrell and the DP's all gathered in front of the door just as the first shot rang out. They each turned to each other with a knowing look. Dontrell put the finishing touches on the door and watched with expectation as it smoothly opened up. They all entered the room with skill and precision, flanking each other and heading towards the loud sounds of gunfire and chaos. The skilled men made eye contact as they moved in that direction. To the right was what appeared to be living quarters, a quick scan proved it to be empty. Patrick and Pennington dropped to one knee near Dontrell and they talked with their eyes. Everyone's eyes were saying let's keep moving forward.

The next room they came to wasn't empty and to Dontrell's dismay he saw his sister struggling to pull herself from the binds that tied her. They all rushed to her as quietly as possible without making their presence known. Dontrell's emotions were conflicted, on one hand he was glad the shot he heard did not end her life; on the other hand, taking a look at Beverly's face and the damage that was done he wanted to murder something.

The approach of the three figures didn't go unnoticed by Beverly. The sound of the gunfire was still heavy in the air. Her first thought was whoever was shooting was coming to kill her. There was nothing she could do other than go out like the soldier she was trained to be, so she turned to face her would be killers. She thought she was hallucinating as she opened her good eye wide and as saw her baby brother and her boys coming towards her. Beverly's mind begin to wonder, how did they? What are they doing together? Words were forming in her brain, but they never reached her lips. Beverly's throat was dry and her nerves were shot. She is a true soldier, but the emotional rollercoaster she has been on tonight is the culmination of years of grief and rage. Dontrell cut the duct tape from her hands and Patrick cut it from her feet as Pennington took up a post at the front of the door. Beverly's eyes held questions that could not reach her mouth. Dontrell pulled her up from the chair and held her close, but she was ripped from his arms by Patrick. Agent Patrick pulled Beverly in close and kissed her so passionately it left no doubt in anyone's mind he was a man in love.

Patrick couldn't explain how seeing her alive and although hurt, was affecting him. He had to express to her what he was feeling in his heart and silently prayed Beverly didn't reject him. Beverly found her voice and looked deep into Patrick's eyes and asked him what took him so long? Patrick assured her he would never be late again. Dontrell cleared his throat ever so lightly to remind Patrick they all needed to move.

As they were retreating Beverly could hear what was going on in the other room. She heard a voice tell the twins they were going to die here today. The voice said the family business would be his as it rightfully should be. Beverly was conflicted. She felt like she should try and save her sisters. The expression on her face was one of pure confusion; she didn't know where this sisterly loyalty was coming from thinking

"These bitches tried to kill me."

But her feet wouldn't move from the spot. She felt as if quick sand had gained control of her feet and she was beginning to sink right where she stood. Dontrell was watching his sister intently wondering why she was hesitant and he started nudging her forward. The look on Beverly's face was in line with her movements, slow and steady, as she mouthed for Dontrell to wait. She then took his gun out of the back of his pants and made her way towards the commotion before either of them could stop her.

Dollar emerged from the shadows and witnessed the look on everyone's face, all of their faces registered pure hatred.

"I DON'T GIVE A FUCK. I told y'all bitches I was coming for ya asses, did you think I was bullshitting?"

Dominique attempted to grab for Dollar and just as he was moving out of her grasp a figure appeared from the hallway and began to fire expertly landing a bullet in Dollar's shoulder almost taking off his head. Dollar felt the slug enter his body as he dodged Dominique and began firing in the direction of the shooter wondering,

"Who the fuck? Oh shit it's the mutherfucking cop, but why the fuck is she trying to help the twins after they beat the shit out of her? "

Everyone in the room began to scramble firing in all directions. The smoke and the multiple bullets were flying over Dollars head making him concede he was out numbered but not outdone. He was not sure if he shot anyone, but he could hear the moaning and screaming as he went into stealth mode to attempt to get behind the shooters.

The twins were pissed their Uncle had taken it this far. Dominique, who was closest to him, was particularly fucked up by his final decision. This was his final decision in her estimation. Attacking the twins and challenging all their father had built would be his last and worst choice, the twins would see to that.

The shooting from the opposite side of the room caught Dominique's attention as Desmond once again shielded her. She made a mental note to explore the possibility of her and Desmond as he pulled her to him and asked,

"Are you good Dom? Can't have anything happening to my baby. "

The look in Desmond's eyes told the story; he was feeling more for her than he was ready to verbalize. One thing for sure, he would not let anything happen to her. Desmond made eye contact with Marcus who was just as protective of Monique. The look that passed between the two men proved to be enough; they knew they would protect these women with their own lives. Desmond nodded his head towards the entrance of the room while they both made haste towards the entrance with their weapons hot, taking care not to get shot along the way.

The twins had the same idea as they teamed up to go after Dollar. Their emotions were high, between their uncle turning on them and Beverly's claims about their father they were operating with an extra level of adrenaline. Monique was volatile, if not more, than Dominique at this point. She had taken a bullet in the leg, that went straight threw, but served as a rally for revenge. She could taste it, she could smell it, and now she had to have it. The twins decided to use the hit him high, hit him low tactic they perfected over the years. Splitting up and going into stealth mode they were able to corner their uncle, giving him only one target, which left him at a disadvantage. Monique aimed her trusted Glock low expertly placing a bullet in Dollar's left bicep.

As he attempted to take cover Dominique skillfully raised her .357 and put another hole in her uncle's chest. They left him slowly bleeding out where he lay and turned to go help their men.

Agent Beverly was not sure why she took the shot that landed in Dollars shoulder, but she was soon back to her senses as she realized the very women she was trying to help were now shooting at her.

"That's what the fuck I get for getting emotional. Fuck them bitches."

She watched as the DP's and her brother tackle with equally skilled killers as she made her way towards the twins to exact her revenge. So many emotions were passing through her as she readied her .10mm to rid herself of GOD's precious daughters just as he had rid himself of her all those years ago.

Agent Beverly didn't go unnoticed by the twins as they all made their way towards each other for the anticipated confrontation each one wanted for different reasons. Beverly felt she would be vindicated. Monique wanted to restore her father's image. Dominique wanted Beverly eliminated from the face of the earth. They all planned on fulfilling their hearts desires as their approached neared.

The twins could tell Beverly was just as deadly as they were. The determination in her eyes, their father's eyes, was equal to their own. Fortitude was a birth right afforded to the Dunbar Klan and it was apparent Agent Beverly was also a recipient, but neither sister was focused on the possibility of a reunion as they simultaneously raised their weapons letting their skill write the ending to the story.

The smell of blood and death was in the air as Dollar regained consciousness. He could hear the gunfire in the distance as he began to prepare his mind to focus on his escape. He had no plans on giving up his claims to the Dunbar Empire but he also knew he needed to retreat so he could regroup to fight another day. Every muscle in his body hurt as he made his move towards the back room he entered through. Dollar silently hoped the twins were dead, but deep inside he knew they were survivors and he would have to eliminate them himself; the Dunbar way.

"Fuck. Fuck. Fuck.. I didn't get to end this like I planned to and now I know what this means; this means war!".

Shoot First Ask Questions NEVER2 Now Available

About The Author

Born and raised in Oakland California, Fanita Pendleton relocated to Norfolk Virginia during her senior year in high school, and has called the magnificent city home ever since. Fanita began her career as a Juvenile Probation Officer and later worked in Adult Probation before taking a short break to pursue her love of teaching as a Criminal Justice Instructor at a local technical college. Recently Fanita stepped back into law enforcement, and is now a Parole Officer.

Fanita blazed on the scene with her Criminal Romance Series: Shoot First Ask Questions Never, Fist Full of Tears and The Moscato Diaries. An avid reader, Fanita holds a special place in her heart for the unsung genre of Urban Crime and Urban Romance Dramas, and in her youth, devoured the works of such greats as Donald Goines, and Iceberg Slim. Fanita is Owner of Urban Moon Books where she is now giving young authors their shot at making their dreams come true.

Fanita received her Master's Degree in Public Administration from Troy University, as well as a Bachelors in Sociology from Langston University, and her Associates in Communications from Luzerne County Community College. She enjoys shooting pool, both for league and leisure, and catching a football, or basketball game with her son, the inspiration of her dreams. Connect with Fanita on Face book "Fanita Moon Pendleton", Instagram #FanitaMoonPendleton, Twitter @Moon081471 or through her website http://www.urbanmoonbooksandmore.com

Books By

Fanita Moon Pendleton

Shoot First Ask Questions Never Parts 1-3

Fist Full Of Tears 1-2

The Moscato Diaries

MOET: Money Over Everything

Open Marriage: A Fatal Attraction Story

Coming Soon

The Moscato Diaries Part 2

MOET Part 2

That Dirty South Love: CoCo's Story

Heirs To The Thrown

56157365R00143

Made in the USA
Columbia, SC
22 April 2019